WORLD WAR II

BOOK ONE

THE RIGHT FIGHT

CHRIS LYNCH

SCHOLASTIC PRESS ★ NEW YORK

Copyright © 2014 by Chris Lynch

All rights reserved. Published by Scholastic Press,
an imprint of Scholastic Inc., *Publishers since 1920.*
SCHOLASTIC, SCHOLASTIC PRESS, and associated
logos are trademarks and/or registered trademarks of Scholastic Inc.

Library of Congress Cataloging-in-Publication
Data Available

ISBN 978-0-545-52294-6
10 9 8 7 6 5 4 3 2   13 14 15 16 17 18
Printed in the U.S.A.   23
First edition, January 2014

The text type was set in Sabon.
Book design by Christopher Stengel

PART ONE
AMERICA

CHAPTER ONE

In the Dugout

There are six teams today in the Eastern Shore Baseball League. Tomorrow there will be none.

The war is changing everything. And we're not even in it yet. We will be. We *should* be. If the big boys asked me, we'd be all the way in already. As of yet, nobody's asked me.

Sure feels like the shift is on, though, from peacetime to wartime. And today has a definite feeling of change about it.

The Sudlersville band is marching around and making noise for us, for the fans, for baseball, for John Philip Sousa, for our way of life, for freedom. Here they come now, right past the dugout, and every man is standing at attention as they go by. They are from Jimmie Foxx's hometown and Jimmie Foxx's hometown is right down the road and they're playing for Jimmie Foxx, who used to play in this very league, if not for this exact team, the Centreville Red Sox. He plays for those other Red Sox now, a little ways north of here. Jimmie Foxx, for crying out loud.

The Sudlersville band is playing for all this and more because today is the last day of the Eastern Shore League season, and this season is the last one until who knows when.

Bigger fish to fry tomorrow. But that's tomorrow. Today, there is no bigger fish than baseball.

The Nazis hate baseball. This I know. And I hate the Nazis. So it is in their honor that I am going to play as hard as I can today, and beat the stuffing out of the Federalsburg A's.

Actually, that's probably the one completely unchanged thing about today. I *always* want to beat the stuffing out of the A's.

I'm sitting in the dugout with Eddie Popowski, who everybody calls "Pop," which is kind of a riot since he's five foot four and he looks young enough that half the guys on the team could be *his* old man. He'll never make it to The Show with that physique. He must have used every trick there is to even get to D-League, which is probably why he has such a sharp eye for every detail of the game. Which is why I sit next to him every chance I get.

"Look at those two guys," Pop says, and with just a little flick of his head I know who he's talking about. The McCallum brothers, who play shortstop and second base for the A's.

"Yeah, Pop, I see them."

"Yeah, you see them. But did you ever see anything *like* them?"

"Maybe," I say coolly, perhaps even childishly.

Pop knows just what I'm up to. He leans away from me and gives me the slicing sideways stare. "Maybe? Roman, you *maybe* saw the likes of these two before? No, sir, you did not. Look at them."

I am looking. They are taking infield practice right now and turning double plays with the kind of effortless grace that makes the batter not even bother running.

"They are like one organism out there," Pop says. "They are a two-headed beast of baseball beauty."

Now I give him the sideways stare.

"I *hate* those guys," I finally confess.

"Yeah?" Pop says, laughing. "Well, you better plan to hate them more, because those guys are going to The Show."

And because Pop is a kind person, he leaves out the ". . . and you're not" part.

But, really, I'm okay with that. I was always border-line as a prospect, anyway, and since I tore up my ankle last season and lost a step or three that I never got back, it's not even a question.

So I'm not quite quick enough for pro ball, but I'm plenty quick enough for the Army. And since it's going to be the United States Army and friends who save the world for baseball, and for every other aspect of the American Dream, I kind of consider this a promotion.

I'd take The Dream over The Show every time.

Mel Parnell comes and sits next to me on the bench. Mel is the tall and jug-eared talent who is pitching for us today. The conversation with Pop hasn't managed to make me any more mature or gracious.

"Mel, would ya be a pal and bean both of the McCallums for me today?"

Mel first grins broadly then drops all serious on me. "What is it about those guys that gets you so riled up?"

"You know what it is?" I say. "No guts. Y'know, they fly around like it's ballet or something, make rou-tine plays look hard. They hotdog it. The shortstop, what's his name . . ."

"Theo," Pop says.

"Yeah, well, he's all spikes when he slides into the

bases, but when somebody tries to take out the other jamoke, what's his name . . ."

"Hank," Pop says.

"Yeah. You try and take him out with a hard slide that isn't even illegal, jeez, you gotta chase the guy into center field before you can even touch him."

They are both laughing at me now. It's not entirely clear if they agree with me or if they're just enjoying my outrage, but I know I'm right. And Pop, anyway, would say something if he disagreed because he doesn't like it any better than I do when guys don't play the game right.

"And that's why you want me to hit 'em," Mel says.

"Yes, please."

"Both of them."

"Yes, please."

Pop slaps me on the back, adds in a little massage thing, too, on my neck muscles like I'm some kind of nut who needs pacifying. "You don't take no prisoners, do ya, kid?"

"No, I don't. And I never will, either. Fight for right. That's the way I look at it. Fight for the things that are right. Otherwise you lose them."

Mel stands all lanky, stretches a bit, starts out of the dugout toward the bull pen. "I gotta go warm up," he says.

"So you'll hit 'em, yeah?"

"No. C'mon, Roman. I'm not one of those guys. I pitch inside when I have to, to keep 'em honest, but I don't throw at nobody on purpose."

"But you're a lefty. Anything can happen with a lefty. They'll just think you went all goofy for a few minutes."

"No," he says, emphatic but not nasty. "But I do admire your passion, Roman, I'll give you that."

"Then give me this. If they crowd the plate, you'll send 'em a message pitch, high and inside. A little chin music is all I ask, for a pal, for the grand old game, for the final day of the Eastern Shore League, and for doing things *right*."

He turns and starts toward the bull pen. "Well, they do tend to hog the plate. Especially that Theo . . ."

Baseball is a tough game. It's an honor game. It's a beautiful game, and this is going to be a beautiful baseball day.

Then I get jolted.

"Did I really just hear you *request* two beanings?"

Startled, I do a sort of hop—midair twist in the direction of the voice. The lovely honey voice, which tells you right away it's not any of the mugs on this team.

"I didn't think you'd come," I say, kinda goofy but so what. "Hannah, I'm very glad you could make it."

"So am I. Only thirty seconds in the dugout and already I know about the violent shenanigans that go on behind the scenes at these clubs."

"Oh, that?" I say, pointing over my shoulder in the direction of today's starting pitcher who is on his way to brush up on his brushback pitch at my request. "That's not violence, that's . . . strategy."

"Hmmm," she says. "Violent strategy."

"No, really. It's just about the unwritten rules, the integrity of the game. It's The Code. And The Code says that guys who spike and hide and don't face the music —"

"The Code also says no dames in the dugout," barks Nardini from the far end of the bench. Nardini is a fine left fielder, a little too pugnacious for his own good, a guy you're usually glad is on your side.

"Hey," I bark back, "this is no dame. This is a *ballplayer*."

I turn and give my girl a big, protective smile, even though we have not quite established that she is my girl.

"Thanks," she says. "I guess."

Hannah is a ballplayer, and a fine one. That's how I found her and how I fell for her, if you want to know the truth. She played right here on this field earlier this year, for the Centreville Ladies in an exhibition match. She played center field better than the guy we have, and went four-for-four, including an inside-the-park home run where she had to bowl over the catcher to score. That was the moment. I knew I was gonna marry her, or try real hard to, anyway, even before I went over like a dumb ol' fan to meet her after the game.

"Looks very much like a dame to me," says Nardini, who is suddenly not at the other end of the dugout. He is right here giving Hannah a close inspection.

I step in between them. "Well, you look like a dame to me, Nardini, and nobody's saying you can't stay."

The guys all burst out in exaggerated laughter, hooting and whistling at Nardini. He's not the hardest guy in the world to get a rise out of, and he gives me a shove. I stumble back, banging into Hannah, then rush to shove Nardini in return. Before it can get too crazy, all the guys are right there with us, separating us, cooling things, making light of it all.

"C'mon, boys," Pop calls loudly, clapping. "Time to take the field. Let's go, let's go."

We scramble for gloves, hats, whatever, bumping into each other, stepping over each other, and then Nardini is back. He's carrying his glove in one hand. He steps right up to Hannah and I tense up until he whips off his hat and does almost a bow.

"Of course you're welcome in our dugout, miss. It's an honor to have you."

She smiles, bows back, and I am just about reappreciating Nardini until he slips me a sneer that says he'd clobber me right now if she wasn't watching.

I have one eye on Nardini, watching him do that distinctive horse-parade high-step run out to his position in left, and I trot to mine at first base. I'm a little disappointed in myself for even letting him distract me this much because at this point, less than a minute after the dustup, I should have forgotten about it already. A little disappointed with myself, and a little impressed with Nardini for his moxie. Nobody else on the team would give me that kind of guff. I'm The Captain.

I don't mean the captain of the team. Well, yes, I do, because I am. I'm captain of this team, as I was captain of last year's team and my high school baseball *and* football teams. It's just how it always is, and everybody has pretty much always called me The Captain. Since, I think, even before high school, though I can't for the life of me remember how that started.

I can say with certainty I was not the best player on any one of those teams. But just as certainly, I was, rightly, The Captain.

I could lie and say that I'm not concerned with the whole Captain business, or that I'm humbled by it. But a true Captain doesn't lie.

I am immensely proud that The Captain is me.

Which is probably why I'm still hanging on a little too much to the Nardini incident, which is unusually undisciplined of me.

Or, maybe . . .

Maybe this is why dames don't belong in dugouts.

CHAPTER TWO

Ball Games

The game itself, for all its significance as the final throw for Eastern Shore League baseball and everything, is kind of not monumental. You might even call it boring, if you weren't an avid baseball fan and a student of the game. I myself happen to be an avid baseball fan and a student of the game, and I'm tempted, anyway.

Parnell, though, is dominating. He's mowin' 'em down at such a clip it's hard to tell whether he's just got the stuff today, or if the A's have already half packed it in for the season. The first two innings pass the same way: three up, three down. Three strikeouts, two weak grounders, and a pop out to the catcher. Ball never gets out of the infield, and the A's look like they aren't really bothered by it. This enrages me. I don't care what game it is. When you play, you *play*, play the game right, show respect, fight through at bats, make the pitcher work, at least, run hard down the line, make something happen. You can put your lazy feet up later.

Not that we're doing a whole lot better. Down in order in the first. Nardini, our cleanup hitter, is in the box now, but he's taken two ugly, undisciplined swings at balls in the dirt. Pitcher then gets comical and throws one about three feet above the strike zone, and I swear Nardini looks like he might go for it before pulling himself together.

"I *hate* that team," I grumble to Hannah, who is sitting next to me on the bench. She's been hunched over, leaning in the direction of the action, charting every pitch.

"What's wrong with you?" she says, still locked on the pitching. Another ball in the dirt fails to tempt Nardini this time and it's 2-2.

"What do you mean, what's wrong with me? Are you blind?"

"Don't talk to me like I'm an umpire."

"Sorry. But it's plain obvious. The A's are laying down. If they're not pulling dirty tricks they're quitting, and I don't know which I hate worse."

Hannah takes a short, irritable break from watching baseball to turn and watch me, with a very scrunched scowl. "Is it about tomorrow?" she says, gradually unfrowning as the words roll out.

It's not. It's about what's right.

"What *it*?" I say. "There is no *it* to be about tomorrow. And no, it's not."

She is still staring at me, with bold, obvious, radiating doubt on her face, when the Federalsburg pitcher finally decides to be a man and challenge Nardini with a fastball in the strike zone. The play takes place behind Hannah but in front of me, and I see her instantly wince at the sound of the murderous crack of the bat. She doesn't even turn to watch as the crowd howls and the ball screeches across the sky to get out of the park in a real hurry.

Nardini is making a show of it, smiling and waving to the crowd as he circles the bases for, who knows, maybe the last time. Everything's like that now, like what's tomorrow gonna bring, and what am I doing right now that I will never do again? A home run is that kind of thing, that'll make a person think a thing like that, and the crowd's reaction sounds like they know it, too.

"Are you not ready for tomorrow, is that it?" says Hannah, one of the world's great baseball fans completely ignoring a quality baseball moment. All the Red Sox are up off the bench hooting and clapping all around us as Nardini tags the plate and trots our way. It's a cozy, odd, isolated moment, Hannah and me alone in the middle of it.

"I'm ready for tomorrow," I say sternly. "I'm ready for every tomorrow. I've been ready for tomorrow forever."

"Oh," she says with an exaggerated sigh and a mocking pat on my knee. "That's much better. I like it when you're a blowhard much better than when you're a grouch."

"I am never a bl —"

"So," Nardini butts in, talking straight to my lady, "what did you think of *that* smash?"

"*That's* blowharding," I say to her, pointing at him.

She ignores me, goes coy with him. "Oh, I'm really sorry, but I was just talking to my gentleman friend here, and took my eye off the ball for a second. Did you do something quite special?" She throws in some rapid blinking for added effect.

This is a perfect woman. This is *the* perfect woman.

He opens his mouth wide to start explaining, but even big ol' dumb Nardini knows that if you have to try and tell the story of a perfectly hit baseball and its trip across the sky, you've already lost. You can never tell the story the ball told itself, and trying just makes it all smaller.

"Sorry," he says politely, "please go back to your discussion."

He does have respect. He's a jerk, but he has respect, or something like it, anyway.

"Maybe I am a little irritable," I say to her. "A little distracted, sure."

As I'm talking, and the usual noisy ruckus of a ballpark roars all around us, Hannah's eyes squint in an amused tight grin, and she covers her chuckling mouth.

"What?" I say, and the roar of the game comes closer and closer until Pop is bellowing in my ear, shoving a bat into my hands.

"You're on deck, ya big knucklehead," he says, grabbing me by the shirt and hauling me up.

There is laughter from the guys all around me, guys slapping my back and poking my sides.

"Dames in the dugout!" Pop calls out, flailing like a little crazy man. "Dames in the dugout! This is why." He stops short. Takes off his hat, speaks like an altar boy to Hannah. "No offense, miss," he says.

"None at all," she says, then flamboyantly spits onto the floor.

"Whoa!" the dugout erupts at the move, and as I am shoved out in the direction of the on-deck circle, I am aware of her having the dugout — my dugout — in the palm of her hand.

I am still thinking it as I take my practice swings. I glance over in her direction, and as soon as I do, she looks at me furiously, waving me away with both hands.

She's completely right. No part of my mind should be in that dugout when I'm about to hit. Jeez, she's a better baseball man than me at this point.

Ed Hall is batting ahead of me and, like always, he's giving the pitcher a heavy time. He never wastes an at bat, and rarely swings at any junk. The pitcher's nibbling, pitching him careful, trying not to get hit, rather than trying to get the guy out. A pitcher deserves what he gets when he takes that approach.

And what he gets is a walk. So there's a man on first when I come up.

I dig in quick, like I always do, one-two-three quick scrapes of the ground with each foot until my spikes grab good, and I'm ready.

Only, apparently, I'm not.

High heat, fastball on the outside corner. Strike one, caught looking.

High heat, fastball on the outside corner. Strike two, caught looking.

Changeup, looking exactly like the guy's fastball delivery, same arm speed and angle, only, here it comes, here it comes . . .

It's about seven miles per hour slower, and I am so early and overaggressive in hacking away at it, I probably have enough time to reset and swing again before it arrives.

There is striking out, then there is *striking out.*

As I trudge the seventy-five miles back to the dugout, the team, and the stadium, are as quiet as they were loud just a couple of minutes before.

He embarrassed me, that pitcher. That mediocre junk merchant made me look like I didn't even belong in the Red Sox system, in the Eastern Shore League, in D-ball at all.

And on that long walk back to the home dugout, I realize he did the right thing. He did exactly what should have been done.

Because I don't belong here.

Batting sixth. Sixth. I have been steadily migrating my way down the lineup this year. Started out batting second. I was never really fast enough to be a leadoff man, so for me, second was top of the order. Then I was moved down. Third, very briefly, as third is usually the spot for your best hitter. Fourth, cleanup, very briefly, as cleanup is usually the spot for your most potent power hitter, and that was always Nardini. But I was The Captain, so if I needed to move into a spot, the spot was mine until I proved that it wasn't. Which I promptly did.

Maybe that's one of the reasons Nardini has a bit of a chip about me. Because they gave me his job, even if only for a while, without my ever earning it.

I'm already getting a little tired of saying this, but maybe Nardini's right.

I keep walking to the dugout. I see it there. I recognize the general outlines of teammates and the completely fine-tuned features of the girl I'm going to marry, and I hear the relentless silence all around. But the dugout is taking forever to get to me.

Then, fifth. Fifth is a good spot to hit, a place I felt comfortable, a place I could do some damage, knock in some runs. Fifth was a good fit.

Then, I blinked, and I was reading the lineup card, and there I was, sixth.

You are not a prospect if you're hitting sixth. You're okay, a decent ballplayer, but not really a threat. You're not one of the guys like shortstops and pitchers they hide at the bottom of the lineup, but you're not far away, either. Guys hitting sixth are on their way up or on their way down, but they are not who a Class D minor league team is really thinking seriously about.

And when you are The Captain, and you used to be a real prospect, and you have cascaded your way down the lineup all year, and now, at lowly sixth, you get embarrassed on three pitches by a guy who's probably already thinking about if his old job on that Chesapeake crabbing boat is still waiting for him, then things are probably happening the way they should. Times and the world and situations are shifting, and if I couldn't pick up the spin on that changeup and know it for what it was, then that is because I am no longer what I have been for a long time: a privileged, lucky guy in spikes and a soft hat, playing games and just hoping that the sun shines today.

I am falling out of baseball, the greatest thing in the world.

But I'm falling up. Into something much, much greater.

The walk, from my humiliation to the dugout of the last game of the 1941 Centreville Red Sox season, is endless but finally ending, and I have again been so caught up in something else that I haven't even realized what I have been looking directly at, what has been ringing in my ears.

They are all up, my teammates, clapping for me. Clapping that clapping where their hands are way high above their heads, like you do for something truly extra special that deserves a higher something than a standing ovation. It's spreading up into the stands, and the fans' appreciation is wonderful, and confusing and stunning, and I'm almost angry because hey, I *struck out*, and did so like a guy who had never seen a baseball before.

But. Oh. Now I get it. I get it that they get it. Word filters, and people know I am switching uniforms for good.

My ankle doesn't allow me to torque into the swing the way I once did. So I'm hedging, guessing, anticipating the pitch, hoping. My average has dropped to .239.

London was bombed, again, mercilessly last week. Rubble. The little kids have all been moved out of the city to places far and wide to be out of the line of fire. There are no kids in London. Here, we're playing baseball. I'm playing baseball. Badly.

The whole crowd is on their feet by the time I reach the dugout. Even the rotten Federalsburg A's are applauding, and that's really giving me the willies.

Fighting for my baseball life is so obviously stupid right now.

Fighting for baseball, though. That I can do. That makes all the sense in the world.

I leave for basic training tomorrow. When I signed up, I scheduled it for the very first day after the season was over. We are not in the war yet. But we should be. I, for one, am going to be well-trained when we get in.

It's really crashing noise as I enter the dugout, but that noise has become a tremendous nothing. Though I'm almost knocked forward onto my face by all the serious poundings on the back, I plow my way right through the onslaught to get to the dedicated follower of the game who is not even supposed to be there. I drop down hard on one knee.

"Marry me," I say, sounding as inhuman as a telephone operator droning, *number, please?*

Hannah looks at me with a startled hop, like her eyes are doing a quick jumping jack. Then, she recoups.

"Sorry," she says, brushing me aside, craning her neck to look around me, "I think Mel Parnell's going to bunt the runner over."

Wow.

I whip around in the direction of the action on the field.

"They're hitting Parnell seventh? They're hitting the *pitcher* right behind *me?*"

"Yes," Hannah says to the back of my muddled, pre-occupied head.

Parnell lays down a textbook bunt. Moves the runner over to second like I was unable to do, and he even beats the throw to first.

There is one out — mine — in the bottom of the second. It's a 1-0 game at the end of the season between the teams that are in fourth and fifth place in the league, a league that isn't even going to exist in a few hours. Suddenly, it's a game. And suddenly, the game seems to matter.

"Yes?" I say, looking back into the openness of her face. "Yes? Really?"

"Yes," she assures me. "You are hitting sixth, and the pitcher is hitting seventh. And he's hitting better than you."

There have always been, in my mind, two complete indignities that might well make life no longer worth living. Those would be: backing down from a righteous fight, and hitting in the bottom third of the order.

I will never back down from a righteous fight. That I can pledge.

As for the other thing . . . I'm dangerously close, and hearing it said back at me out loud is somehow even more demoralizing than I had braced for. Not to mention she has completely bypassed the other small question I was asking.

"And, yes," she says, brushing me aside once again.

The eighth hitter is our catcher, Brock, who is a wonderful guy, has twice brought huge pans of an amazing penuche fudge made by his mother that we all devoured like locusts on a field of wheat. He handles the pitching staff like a magician, and would be a dynamic hitter, if the rules were changed to make the ball four times its current size. He simply cannot hit professional-level pitching with any consistency.

First pitch, he makes contact, which was his assignment, and lofts a lazy but useful fly ball to right field. Both runners tag up and advance safely.

Two outs, runners on second and third. Suddenly, all the guys who are not expected to produce are finding the grit and moxie to get the job done in the best baseball scratching and clawing I have seen in a very long time. They are finally acting like the next run matters. In this game. Now.

The game is transformed, like everybody somehow now understands. It's exciting, stupid exciting.

Ninth batter. Our shortstop, Corky, who plays the position like a spider plays flies. Nothing gets by him.

Plays his position as well as it is possible to play it. So why does he seem so surprised and befuddled every time a pitcher throws a ball in his direction? Guys named Corky can never hit.

"Did you say you will marry me?" I say to Hannah.

"I would have a better chance of driving in those runners than that kid does," she says.

"Yes," I say, urgently, "but . . ."

"Pay *attention*," she says, turning me in the direction of the action.

Since I have no choice, I watch the action despite the action being no action at all. The pitcher overwhelms Corky with one fastball, then blows a second straight past him. At least the kid is going down swinging, if that's what you want to call it. Pitcher winds up and we all await the inevitable fastball and the accompanying pleasant breeze to be caused by Corky's helpless swatting at it.

Except of course this day is different, and Corky sort of throws himself and his bat out over the plate and the ball bumps into the bat and the right fielder is caught by such surprise that he's not even started his run in when the ball just makes it over the first baseman's reach and nestles into the shallow outfield grass without even a bounce. The runner on third scores, then the runner on second chugs around and scores without drawing a throw. Corky has delivered, the crowd goes delirious, and this final baseball game is now three to nothing in the hands of the good guys.

I turn back around to Hannah, feeling so triumphant and full of the rightness of things I make my approach a second time, more forcefully, back on my knee but not back on my heels this time.

"Marry me, Hannah," I say.

She looks down at me with a squint of conflict crisscrossing her features.

"How can I do that at this point? As of now, you're officially the worst hitter on the team."

This is getting really rough.

"For goodness' sake, marry the poor guy," Popowski says.

"Can I wait 'til the end of the inning and see if Corky asks me first?" she says.

My knee is starting to hurt. Not as much as my pride, however.

"Sounds fair to me," Pop says graciously.

I remain on my knee while play resumes and Hannah acts all engrossed. I do not take my eyes off her face as she eyes the action. But she cannot suppress a sweeping beautiful smile, and both her hands reach out to take both of mine.

The excitement of the moment catches on, reaching all the way out onto the field, where Corky cannot contain himself, tries to steal second on the first pitch, and is thrown out.

"Well," Hannah says, "I suppose you'll do, then. That was horrible baserunning."

I have to confess that focus is a struggle by the time I take up my position at first base again. I am thinking of bigger things, of reporting for duty, and of engagement to Hannah, her waiting for me while I am away in the Army, and really it is time for this game and this season to be over, so we can make the world safe for all the other games and all the other seasons.

But then come the McCallums.

Ground ball, slap hitters, the both of them, which is why *they* hit, deservedly, at the bottom of the order, seventh and eighth, and why it's taken so long for them to come up to bat. Up first is Theo, the shortstop. Suddenly, focus doesn't seem to be a problem for me. I crouch in anticipation, watching Brock setting up behind the plate and calling for an inside fastball. Parnell goes into his windup.

But Parnell seems to be having control issues. First pitch is outside. Second pitch is in the dirt.

Come on, Mel, look at him crowding the plate. He's owning it. Take it back, send him a little chin music. Go after him, it's your right.

Third pitch is a big looping curveball that fools Theo completely, leaving him flailing and almost falling. It was a fine pitch. But it was not inside, and now Theo McCallum is digging those spikes right back in, crowding home plate like he holds the mortgage on it.

"Time!" I yell to the umpire as I stride across to the mound.

Normally, conferences at the mound are called by the catcher or the coach. But I am still The Captain after all, and this needs to be addressed.

"What's up, Cap?" Mel says.

Brock has come trotting out, too. "Yeah, Roman, what's the problem?"

"We need to pitch him inside."

"But I have him where I want him."

"Where you want him is off the plate. You let him stay where he is and I promise he'll have you. Trust me on this."

The two of them exchange looks, like they know better, but I'm The Captain, right?

We take our positions again. Mel winds up and sends another off-speed pitch out over the plate. Theo attacks it, and slashes a line drive right over my head that thankfully lands foul by a foot.

Parnell half looks at me, and I growl, loud enough for pretty much every guy on the field to hear.

Windup, pitch, sizzling fastball.

Plunk. Ouch. Right in the ribs. That was not exactly the plan. He was just supposed to brush the guy back, get him uncertain. Theo pauses for several seconds, a little hunched over, before dropping the bat and trotting to first.

"You all right, kid?" I say as I stand next to him at the bag. It's a professional courtesy, as I'm not all that concerned.

He says nothing. I hold him close to the base as Parnell winds up and throws the first pitch to his brother.

Same pitch, same speed, same spot, only Hank hits the deck before he can get hit. Guys on the Federalsburg bench start barking, some of our guys bark back. Parnell ignores them, winds up, and comes hard inside again.

Hank is ready, though, and fists a grounder to the left side of the infield. Our third baseman scoops it up and fires to second to start the double play. Only the ball and Theo McCallum reach the second baseman at the same time, and Theo hits the guy like it's a football tackle, driving his shoulder into our guy's hip, and sending him head over heels through the air and hard into the dirt. There is no double play. Hank is already safe at first. I don't even know where the ball has gone, but it doesn't matter.

We have a rhubarb.

Nardini is somehow the first guy to get to Theo McCallum, bombing in from left field. The two of them are locked in a kind of death-grip grapple, rolling into the outfield trying to get a decent shot at each other. I run in their direction as I realize both benches have cleared. Coaches and umpires are trying to get between guys, punches are flying, big haymakers, and it's difficult to even tell who's hitting who. Nardini is on top of Theo and then another guy jumps Nardini from behind so I hustle to help.

Then, I'm on my face with a mouthful of turf. I'm rocking and bucking to try and get the jerk off of me but he keeps jamming my head down and I'm getting nowhere until, suddenly, somewhere, I find the strength to flip him and send him flying.

I jump up and turn around to find it wasn't me flipping him after all.

"Hannah!" I shout, horrified.

She has Hank McCallum from behind, a pretty solid choke hold around his throat with her forearm.

"Ain't hittin' no dame," he croaks, his eyes bulgy and his face red with probably some mixture of embarrassment, outrage, and, well, strangulation.

"Hannah," I say again, rushing up and prying her loose, bundling her back toward the dugout.

The fight is petering out, guys mostly shoving and puffing up at each other. There is shouting — some of it aimed in my direction — but cooler heads are prevailing. If heads that will brawl in such a meaningless situation can ever be called cool.

I'm actually laughing by the time Hannah and I sit on the bench together.

She turns a furious glare on me that stops the laughter like I've been corked. I can smile, though. "The Fighting Bucyks," I say, nodding big approval. "I like it."

She acknowledges my wit with a frown and nothing else. She reaches up to her neck, pulls something out from under her blouse and up over her head like a necklace or dog tags.

"You have to wear this," she says, holding it draped over her fingers for me to see.

"What is it?"

"It's a scapular. If I'm going to wait for you, you're going to wear this for me."

I take it from her and examine it more closely. It's a portrait of Christ, on a one-inch square of fabric, strung with a thin strip of the same stuff. Her face is pinched and serious as she looks back and forth between Jesus's face and mine.

I slip it over my fat head — it's a close call whether it'll get down, but, success.

Her face unpinches. She smiles. She reaches out and gently flicks away some small pieces of turf from my lips.

Nardini adds absolutely nothing to the moment when he plunks down on the bench on the other side of Hannah.

"Hey," he says, like nothing unusual has happened. "Game's starting back up."

"Argh. Hannah, I gotta —"

"No, you don't," Nardini says. "You're ejected."

"What? I didn't even —"

"Yeah, right, neither did I. That's why I'm ejected, too. If it's any consolation, there aren't any McCallums left in the game, either."

"Well," I say, "I suppose it is."

The game retakes its shape, and the Eastern Shore League resumes its steady march to the conclusion, with me as a spectator. Never would have seemed right before. But it is now.

"This is kinda cozy, huh?" Nardini says, scooting a bit closer to my Hannah.

"The fighting might not be over yet," I growl.

"Ya think not?" he says, scanning the field obliviously for trouble spots. Hannah elbows me playfully.

The game eventually does end, as all games eventually do.

It's a quiet end, the A's going down without a fight, so to speak. Once the McCallums were out of it that was pretty much guaranteed. There is no attempt at players shaking hands. They just turn to their respective dugouts to pack it in. The crowd applauds enthusiastically, on their feet and loud because a Centreville crowd appreciates. Then, unexpectedly, the Sudlersville marching band is fired up and marching back in from right field, while over the crackly, tinny Tannoy public address system, a deep baritone somebody tries to sound important about something.

We've only heard the Tannoy a couple of times this year, once for the owner's birthday and again when there was a fire under the grandstands, and this is a good reminder why. Sounds like somebody's jamming a microphone through a sausage grinder and coughing through it at the same time.

"It's the mayor," Hannah says excitedly. She's a life-long Shore girl and would know if the mayor came around for just any old thing. So I'd say this counts for something. I join her up out of the dugout and on the field.

Through the crackle and over the band, we can just about make it all out.

". . . And while we all have high hopes for the resumption of Eastern Shore League baseball sometime in the future, there are far more serious matters in the world at the present time. So as we say farewell to the boys for now, could I ask the crowd to join me in saluting those brave men on the field today who have already enlisted in our armed services in anticipation . . ."

The Centreville crowd is already way ahead of the mayor, which honestly isn't a huge accomplishment but it's nice. I clap right along with them, clapping for the idea itself rather than clapping for myself. Myself, I'm a little embarrassed and wanting this to be over —

"Go!" Hannah says, shoving me hard in the middle of my back, toward the mound.

"What?"

The mayor is soldiering on, but I need Hannah's translation.

"They are calling you out to the mound. Go."

"Aww," I say, looking at the ground, kicking the dirt like a surly kid. She shoves me again.

I have my head down all the way out there, because this is embarrassing. The crowd goes thunderous, doing the work of a population a hundred times bigger.

It's all still too much and I still have not lifted my head by the time I reach the mound and walk, face-first, into Theo McCallum.

He is enjoying it. Grinning slyly at me, waving at the fans. His brother is right next to him, doing likewise. I look at the group, a mix of both teams that would just about add up to one full squad. A pretty good squad, too, as it happens.

"Hey, look at that pretty gal over there, unescorted," says Nardini, brushing me aside to get a better look at my fiancée.

"I'll have you know, pal," I say to him, gesturing with my thumb toward Hannah, "that's what I'm fighting for. That, and baseball."

All three of them start laughing, climbing over each other to rib me.

"From what I can tell," Hank says, "*that* can take care of itself just fine."

"But if *baseball* is depending on you for survival, we've all played our last game."

That was my own left fielder. He comes up and gives me a hard backslapping hug, whispering deep in my ear, "Just kidding. Go get 'em, Captain."

I go around shaking hands with the other men who've joined up. Some of them marginal talents or worse, some of them mighty fine prospects who have every chance of making it to the bigs. I try not to wonder how many of them will never step on a baseball diamond again.

The band plays on, and the crowd cheers on, as the benches of both clubs gradually start emptying away.

"Hey," Hank McCallum says, grabbing my hand and pumping hard, "that conference you called on the mound . . ."

"Oh, yeah, about that . . ."

"Personally, I thought it was about time." He points a thumb at his brother. "I'd have dropped this scrub on the seat of his pants with the second pitch."

Theo barges in between us. "I wouldn't even have waited that long. But that's Red Sox for ya, not really famous for their bravery, right?"

I shake, grin, grip his hand hard while he does the same.

"What's your branch?" I ask him.

"Air Corps," he says, puffing and pumping.

"And yours?" I ask his brother.

"Navy."

"*Now* it all makes sense," I say, laughing. "Me, I'm Army. When war does break out, I'll let you guys know how it was."

Nardini's apparently feeling left out. "Isn't anybody gonna ask me what —"

"Marines!" we all shout at the same time.

Nardini looks genuinely spooked. "How in the world did you all figure that out?"

"Some things are just too right to be wrong," I say.

It has the feel of some kind of tribute now, some kind of major public reward for something we haven't even done yet, and it's great and all but it needs to be over. One by one, guys make their way down off the mound, across the field, toward their assignments. The band finally peters out. One guy, a talented pitcher for the A's who everybody always seems to be talking about but nobody ever seems to be talking to, strays across the infield between us and the plate. He's carrying a bag. He was not one of the enlistees.

"Oh, look," says Theo. "There goes the phenom. The healthy young man who's planning to play *our* game while we do *his* fightin'."

"What's your problem, anyway?" Hank McCallum shouts at his now-former teammate.

The guy keeps his head down and tries to keep walking.

"Hey!" Theo shouts, in the kind of tone you don't ignore.

"This could be my chance," the kid says shyly. "It's been my dream, always. And with the talk going around — big-time players like Hank Greenberg, the DiMaggios, talk of all those guys signing up . . . guys like me might have a chance they'll never have again."

It is not an irrational thought. But it is a sickening one.

Hank McCallum just manages to tackle his brother as Theo bullcharges in the kid's direction, screaming seven kinds of hate and disgust as the kid turns scarlet and backs away.

"Maybe there won't be any more chances, ever again, for anybody," Nardini calls after the kid. "Ever think of that?"

He steps quicker and quicker to get away.

"Nazis hate baseball!" I shout.

The McCallums, still tangled on the ground, look up at me like I just came down from the mountaintop with The Word. They point at me, and nod agreement.

"Nazis hate baseball," Nardini says, punching my shoulder and marching away as if he just saw a squad of them turning the corner.

"Nazis hate baseball," Hank says, dragging his brother toward their side of the field and beyond.

"Nazis hate baseball!" Theo shouts to the sky.

"Where'd you get that information?"

I turn to see Hannah on the mound next to me. The park is rushing to quiet as we stand face-to-face.

"Oh, they came through here last year with a barnstorming team. You could tell they hated every minute of it. That's when I realized there's something wrong with those guys."

She smiles and touches both of my cheeks lightly with flat palms. "You coming?"

She's going home. Home, Maryland, the Shore. Home, right up the street, in fact. Myself, I go straight from here to the train station, ride back to Boston tonight. Pack up, eat a little, sleep even less, then get on with it.

"Maybe we should leave it here for now, huh?" I say.

"Sounds like exactly what we should do," she says. "Right here. This field. For now."

"You go. I'm going to wait a little longer. Train's not for a bit yet . . ."

"And you want the park to yourself."

"Well, sorta."

"Last man standing," she says, walking backward off the mound, letting her hands slip off my cheeks.

"Last man standing," I say.

I watch Hannah walk across the park, out the gate, up the street. I watch her every step until she turns that corner where I can no longer see her.

Then I turn in the other direction, survey all three hundred and sixty degrees of the old ballpark: empty, mine, cool, quiet. I look up into the dusking sky, raising my left hand straight up and my right hand out to my side as if I'm calling for a high, high fly ball. It's mine. I got it.

CHAPTER THREE

War Games

I've been in two war zones since the last time I stepped onto a baseball field. The only problem is, they weren't in Europe or Asia, they were in the Carolinas and Louisiana. It sounds like the Civil War broke out again, but fortunately that's not it. Though, *un*fortunately, it did consist of Americans fighting Americans. And not even fighting. Sort of fighting. Practice. Rehearsal. War games. *Maneuvers* is what they are officially known as, but it makes no difference what they're called because they are all the same thing: the wrong conflict, in the wrong place, against the wrong guys.

No Nazis. Not one, as far as I could tell.

I did *not* come here to play fight. No, sir.

That's not entirely fair. But I'm not in a fair mood, to be honest, because I feel like I'm a hunting dog that's been trained to the maximum of his abilities and then kept locked up while all the rabbits and foxes and pheasants are running circles around my cage.

The maneuvers were fine, actually, even stunning in a way. Four hundred thousand soldiers, fifty thousand vehicles, a total maneuver area of over three thousand, four hundred square miles of river and plain and swamp and trail and muck and what I came to understand as Louisiana *steam*, all designed to test the physical and mental and spiritual endurance of any fighting man of any era. It was, we were told, the largest peacetime exercise in American history. We learned to coordinate infantry and airborne with armor in a way the Army had never done before. We learned our gear, our machines, the way an old cavalry guy — the guy who was basically losing his place in history to me — learned his horse. It was exciting and sweaty and demanding, and it did make you think things through and really learn the craft of mechanized warfare.

But no Nazis.

It was for the brass, the men at the top of the food chain, more than anything. They were just figuring this kind of warfare out. Guys like me would do whatever they told us, so these exercises were all about them figuring out what to tell us.

I knew it was important, because of the stars involved. There were a lot of West Point types, brainy and gritty lieutenant colonels who were probably going to figure out the whole war in Europe right here in deepest-south USA, and then lead us over there to give the mongering maniacs all the what for they deserve.

But still, no Nazis.

And no real fighting. Blank shells and rounds replaced the real thing, smoke canisters were popped absolutely everywhere, and planes dropped bags of white sand in place of bombs. They even employed loudspeakers to blast battle sounds, presumably from real battles. Triumph was achieved by surrounding troops rather than attacking them, and my favorite element of all: Umpires told us what was what.

Umpires decided who was a casualty, who was captured, who won the battle. The only element of baseball I ever hated, and the only one that followed me into the Army.

I know I learned a lot. I know the Army learned a lot, since they seemed to have had very little idea before the Louisiana Maneuvers of how to integrate the awesome power and maneuverability of the perfect, perfect war machine into their game plan. The tank is war in its best, distilled form. War has been waiting for the tank, forever, since war was born. And since war was born essentially the moment Mr. Ug #1 encountered Mr. Ug #2 sniffing around his food and his Mrs. Ug #1, it is fair and logical to say that humanity has been waiting for the tank to come along since the beginning of thought, and suspicion, and anger, and violence. The tank is the solution to all that. The tank is the Jim Thorpe of mechanization. And Jim Thorpe, American Indian hero and the greatest athlete who ever lived, is pretty much what God would like to be when he grows up.

I understood all along that the maneuvers were a necessary step on the way to what really mattered. But I was also aware, on a day the umpire informed me and the other four crew members of our tank that we had been disabled, that the Germans were in the process of *disabling* Leningrad beyond recognition. Blank ammo, at that moment, was a good idea, since me shooting an umpire would not have solved much of anything.

By the time we got to the Carolina Maneuvers, you could feel the urgency of things, pushing us all to a greater understanding of tank and artillery warfare. Three hundred and fifty thousand troops mock-fought it out over ten thousand square miles between Fort Jackson and Fort Bragg. For me personally it meant a rapid uptick in my grasp of all the skills required on tank duty.

My official assignment was assistant driver, and that was a comprehensive education all itself. I also did duty as a gunner and a loader as required, but Carolina was where I was given an opportunity to take over driver duties more and more, and it was where it became obvious to one and all that I belonged at the controls.

It was still just war games, but when the moment came to show the horse — the tank — that I was a true cavalryman, even the boss had to take notice.

"Bucyk!" yelled Sergeant Boyd, our tank commander.

"Yes, sir?" I yelled back, louder, because I was still so shot through with excitement.

"Where did you learn to do that?"

"Don't know, sergeant. Just seemed like the thing to do, I guess."

What I'd done was this: As we came over a hill and barreled down a ravine, we unexpectedly encountered one of the big beast M-6 heavy tanks of the other side, moving slowly across a stream. Without even thinking about it, I gambled that they hadn't seen us and headed straight for them. My tank, the M-3 Lee, did not have the firepower to slug with those guys and the day would be over real quick if I didn't get tricky.

I hauled tail down there, angling to come right up to their flank as they made it to the other side of the stream where the beginnings of a wood appeared. They saw us just as they entered the first thicket of pines. The M-6 tried to maneuver, but it's an unwieldy brute, and that's the M-3's one area of advantage. I stayed on their flank, making them turn all the way around to try and get a bead on me with the big gun, until I'd twisted them right up. They wound up pressed to a big ol' spruce. The turret spun around after us, but I swung around the other way again, and the big gun banged right into that tree, unable to follow any further when we fronted them and did a full turn right in their face. They were ours. Umpire, please.

"Great going, Bucyk," the sergeant said. "I think you might have a future with this stuff."

"Thanks," I said. And I had a pretty good feeling that my days as an assistant driver were not going to be long.

"Outta my seat," snapped Coulson, the driver.

So, by Carolina, we had progressed a lot, as soldiers, as an army, as a nation. Tank warfare, which was just taking shape at the end of World War I, was obviously going to be front and center this time around.

But as fast as we were evolving, it became clear during those three weeks that the mobile anti-tank artillery that the infantry was using were going to be huge problems for mechanized divisions like us. You'd have to say, even, that they got the better of us in this staged war and word was out that they were now figuring large in the upcoming real thing. Older generals and other brass from older wars were found to be a step slow and an idea short during this exercise. So, as November ended and December 1941 came up, all kinds of changes were happening, with the new regime being all about mobility; integrated units of infantry, artillery, and armor operating seamlessly; and above all, aggression.

We were even in *Life Magazine*. All over it. The country was watching us, like we were actually doing something beyond pretend, and apparently the country was impressed.

But I still couldn't help feeling that, as much as we were learning in Louisiana and East Texas, in Kentucky and the Carolinas, it wasn't nearly as much as the Nazis were learning in Poland and Czechoslovakia, in France, in Norway and Denmark, and the Soviet Union.

Carolina Maneuvers ended on November 30. One week later, we arrived back at Fort Knox, on December 7.

That same day, the world and its war got tired of waiting for us. The Japanese bombed Pearl Harbor, and the myth of American neutrality sank along with more than two thousand sailors.

Thanks to the Japanese, I was going to get my Nazis.

CHAPTER FOUR
Time Waits

Even with the official declaration of war, it somehow still takes an eternity to get into it.

Four months after Pearl Harbor, we were ordered to Fort Dix, New Jersey. Still no Nazis, though there was one guy, a barber, whose behavior really had me wondering. Anyway, it felt a bit closer. Then, a month later, we got *the* call. We were shifted to New York's Brooklyn Army Terminal. From there, we sailed for Europe.

That's how I find myself standing on the top level of probably the most famous and classy ship in the entire world.

The *Queen Mary*.

I never, ever, in any corner of my imagination would have put this vision together for myself.

And at the same time, all things considered, it makes as much sense as anything else.

So much has happened already since the last time I stepped off a baseball field, I feel like I should be seventy years old and telling it all to my grandkids. If I thought it was going to be a relatively straight line from off of that mound in Maryland to the Army to the inevitable war, then I thought altogether wrong. While I've been training, practicing, maneuvering for the better part of a year, the Nazis have been playing for real, dominating, spreading carnage, and rewriting maps, with what seems to be only feeble resistance along the way.

Okay, maybe that's unfair. But they need us over there. They need *me*. I feel that need, and it hurts to think of what help we could be, what our absence has cost already. And now we're going, finally.

I'm taking with me a few things I didn't have before my induction and basic training and Fort Jackson and Fort Knox and the *Queen Mary*. I am bringing a surgically repaired ankle that needed a minor procedure after I took on an obstacle course with more gusto than sense. I'm taking a professional soldier's understanding of the art of warfare, and a scientific assessment of my aptitude that indicated I am more suited to tank duty than I ever was to baseball or school or jumping jacks or tying my shoes or eating ice cream or anything else. I think they even took an X-ray of my skull and found that my brain was tank-shaped. Which means I am also bringing with me my assignment as driver on a five-member crew operating a Sherman M-4, which is waiting for me at the other end of this boat ride. And I am bringing with me something of a hobby in history and conflict that I got a taste for when laying up waiting for my ankle to heal. I believe I learned just enough to understand this war. And I believe I learned enough to expect I'll understand nothing, once I'm in it.

And I'm bringing a new tattoo.

I got it during one of the slow periods at Fort Jackson. A bunch of the guys were going together to get them done, and I just got in step without a lot of thinking about it. A soldier's mentality, I guess you might say. Most of the guys got pretty girls inked on their arms, or somebody's name, or American flags or military insignia. I didn't want to be thinking that way with something that was going to be on my body forever, representing a statement about me, forever. There would be other times, other tattoos, and then maybe *MOM* or Betty Grable or *Old Ironsides* — the Armored Division's nickname — might be right. But this time, it had to be special, a symbol of what I found important and worthy of space on my body indefinitely.

Jim Thorpe. As soon as I started giving this tattoo some thought, the image of Jim Thorpe burst its way into my mental field of vision and wouldn't budge.

It would be hard to overstate my admiration and respect for Jim Thorpe. Olympic champion, professional baseball player, professional football player, a soft-spoken, dignified man who also happens to be a marauding, speedy, powerful force of nature. And, he is a proud American Indian man. We both have some Indian blood and some European, and that is one reason I've found myself so drawn to him and his story since I first heard of him. A great man. He has never let me down.

I was almost convinced that that was my tattoo by the time we got to the parlor. There are several famous images of Jim, so surely there wouldn't be a problem finding one. Maybe in his Cleveland Indians cap. Jim Thorpe *and* baseball might represent me just dandy.

I sat in a grubby little waiting room with three other guys while three more were ushered right in. They should have offered a military discount, because we seemed to be completely supporting the place. There were samples all over the walls, the usual stuff, ships and anchors and mermaids and snakes and dragons, but as I stared around and around at them I noticed one of Mount Rushmore, too. Wasn't expecting that. Then, a series of Wild West–themed designs.

To their credit, the proprietors had it all covered, the cowboy stuff, Buffalo Bill and all that, the great train robbery stuff, the Civil War. They had one design with generals Lee and Grant somehow both up close in the same frame, and smiling. I don't know who the person is who might have bought that one but I believe I would like to meet him. Once.

They gave the American Indian a sizable presence there, even if a lot of it was that unfortunate whoop-whoop savage stuff that probably doesn't represent anybody who ever lived. They had blondie General George Custer, too. Every American kid knows the bloody mess that was Custer's Last Stand, but I'd bet fewer folks appreciate that before that fiasco he was a fine cavalry officer who was on the right side of things at Gettysburg and Appomattox. Certainly fewer still would know that there is convincing evidence — I'm convinced by it, anyway — that I am distantly related, on my mother's side, to both Custer *and* his noble nemesis, Lakota Sioux Chief Sitting Bull. And there he was, the next image over from Custer, staring him down like he'd like to get another crack at him right now.

My family has always done their part in this country's military, going back to every single scrap even before the Revolution. I come from warriors, and I'm proud of that.

The only part of that history that hurts my heart is the Indian Wars.

"Time waits for no man, and neither do I!" bellowed the tattoo artist as he thumped back into the waiting room with yet another sore-armed soldier trailing behind him. It was the third time I'd heard this same announcement, so I figured time had come for me.

"So why'd you choose this one?" my pal Pacifico shouts over the raw wet wind and the great ship's slowing engines. He and I met while killing time — and nothing else — in Fort Knox. We worked out that it appeared we would be assigned to the same unit. He seems to have interpreted that to mean the two of us *are* a unit, since he's everywhere, every time I turn around. I don't mind, actually. The *Queen Mary* — I'll never get used to that — is approaching Belfast Harbour and the next little jump in our long hopscotch to war. Pacifico saw the lower edges of my forearm tattoo as I leaned heavily over the rail — as if I could get us there that much faster by shoving us there. I pull up the sleeve and he traces the great chief's contours with his finger.

"Because Jim Thorpe is still alive, and I think it's a little strange to have a live guy on your arm. I'm pretty sure Jim doesn't have a tattoo of me — yet — but I could be wrong."

"Yu-huh," he says. "That explains why Jim isn't here. Now how come Sitting Bull is?"

We got along pretty smooth from the minute we met, me and Pacifico. I think we could just recognize something in each other that makes it easy, makes us be able to say anything to each other at any time. If we feel like saying anything at all. Which lots of times we don't, and that's also hunky-dory, especially if we'll be spending lots of time cooped up in the same tank, with three other guys.

He's been well aware of the tattoo all along but never asked. Suddenly, it's very interesting to the guy, as Northern Ireland, and mainland Europe there hiding behind it, is sailing right for us.

There it is. It's coming into view now.

"Long time between question and answer, Bucyk. Is

it an unbearable, shame-based answer, is that it? Will it make you cry?"

He knows that Sitting Bull, the real one, would cry before I would. Probably the tattoo one, too.

"Family," I say, evenly but in a voice that I hope signals this is a no-joke area.

"Honest Injun?" he says, dumb enough to violate my warning voice but wise enough to be backing away as he does it.

"I played pro ball, Pacifico. I'm pretty sure I could reach that ice-cold water if I threw you from here."

He has a big meaty grin that somehow doubles the size of his face. He's also undoing his jacket and his shirt as he comes closer again.

"Seriously, though," he says, "you Indian, Bucyk? What kinda Indian tribe does *Bucyk* come from?"

"My father's tribe," I say sarcastically. "They come from Ukraine. Indian's from my mother's people."

"Ukraine," he says earnestly. "Is that a country or something?"

It's not the first time I have wondered how much of the world's geography most of us only know through wars. But it is the first time I feel there's something I can do about it.

"I have a really, really long answer to that. Or, a short one."

He is politely diplomatic. "Maybe the short one for now. Then the long one for when we have more time."

"It is a country. Though for centuries a lot of invaders have failed to respect that. Including Uncle Joe Stalin now."

"Hey," he says, actually looking around like a teacher might hear and we'll get in trouble. "That's an ally you're talking about."

"Oh, I know," I say. "I've been following the news of all those brave Russians fighting off the Nazis in Stalingrad."

"Right. Heroes."

"Yeah, except that about a third of the heroes forgot to tell the Russians they are Ukrainians."

There is a little bit of thoughtful silence now.

"This is the short version, Bucyk, yeah?"

I have to laugh. "Ah, yeah, I guess. Sorry."

"Uh-huh . . . So, your mom's an Indian. Well, I think that's great, pal," he says as he struggles with a stuck zipper and then frozen fingers that don't manage buttons too nimbly. "And I think that you're great for honoring family."

He lets out a little yip of triumph when he manages to defeat the fiercely resistant buttons, and I wonder briefly what he'll make of real battle. Then he opens the curtains, exposing his chest to me and the bracing wet cold, but he is undeterred as he seems to be generating his own heat, from his core.

Nonna it says, arched, gold with orange and red like a sunrise over his left pectoral. The script is calligraphy or something, real art, and probably cost him twice the bucks, twice the pain, and twice the time in the chair that I had to spend.

I smile and nod and stare just the way I am surely supposed to, and finally I tell him it is beautiful because that's just what it is.

"*Nonna*," he says, still chipper and proud but finally conceding to cold reality as he covers back up. "It's Italian for grandmother. It's for my *nonna*."

You cannot help smiling goofy with a guy who is smiling at you so powerfully goofy right there. It has the power of a small sun or something and you just cannot fight it.

The *Queen Mary* blasts its world-shaking horns as we pull into Belfast Harbour where it looks like the entire population of the island is there shouting for us, and almost as many of our guys are crowding the decks to holler right back at them.

"You're a good boy, Pacifico," I say as I wave both hands overhead at the folks who are all waving at us just like that.

"She's a good *nonna*," he replies, waving the same waves at the same folks.

The cheering from these people, from these foreign people, is overwhelming. I never lacked for motivation or desire to get in on the right fight, but this is stirring me up in a whole new frenzy for it. They are cheering so mad and so certain even though they don't even know us, even though we haven't done a blessed thing yet, for them or for anybody else.

But we're gonna. I guarantee right now, we're gonna.

Endurance. That's what we learn during our extended time training in Northern Ireland. We learn to endure endless waiting, which obviously features large in the Army experience. But we also learn to endure abysmal weather conditions, lashing sideways rain for days and days on end while we practice maneuvers out in mucky bogs that make tank movement a serious challenge. Like the rain here, I find myself driving sideways as much as straightways, but I have to admit this part of training has done as much for my skills as anything else so far. The Sherman M-4 is bigger and heavier than the M-3 I first learned on, and the driver sits a lot lower, too, so I am happy enough to get in every extra hour, in all kinds of slop, in order to become fully a part of the machine.

The other great benefit to our time here is getting to know the other parts of the machine.

The tank crew, that is. It's a unit that, by design, has to operate as closely and interdependently as any in the military.

Our tank commander, a captain, is named Cowens. He is the most vital part of this machine, and you can see that within seconds and without him having to tell you. Though he is perfectly happy to tell you, if you require telling. And he's happy to tell you that you require telling. He's older than the rest of us by a few years, probably pushing thirty, and is so invested in every aspect of what he calls Tanking, Tankery, The Art of Tankism, Tank-you-very-much — really pretty much anything you can bend the word *tank* into — that I wonder if he'd even be here if they used tanks in farming or whaling or lumberjacking. I think he'd be happiest if he could just have his own tank, roaming the globe with it as the world's deadliest private citizen. I've never been afraid of any man — not bragging, just revealing — but if I were going to be, I suppose I'd start with him.

I'm the driver, of course, with Pacifico, my right-hand man, as assistant driver and machine gunner. Up in the turret with Commander Cowens are the main gunner, Logan, who mans the big 75-mm cannon, and the loader, Wyatt, who keeps that weapon and all the rest fed and ready for action.

We get to know one another steadily throughout the Northern Ireland training, but it all comes together one night when we are required — forced — to stay out on maneuvers, and the rain and sleet and wind and freezing temperatures keep us bunked down in the Sherman overnight, supposedly to sleep.

Sleeping upright is bad enough, but the tank is *cold*. There is one surface that's like a shelf over the engine compartment that retains some warmth for a while even after the engine is shut down. We arrange a rotation where we switch and take turns up there periodically, but it becomes obvious that staying bundled up in your seat beats moving around and climbing up there for the increase of maybe one degree of heat you get out of it.

"First Armored Division," Commander Cowens growls into the dark as the rain's million billion Irish dancers go on with the show.

It sounds like some kind of challenge, and for several long seconds nobody wants to pick it up. I figure ignoring him would probably be a worse option so I decide to take one for the team and respond.

"Quite an honor, I'd say," I say.

"Quite a joke, actually," he answers. His tone comes down some and it sounds more like he's getting something off his chest, or educating some rookies, than picking a scrap. "The Second Armored Division is the real McCoy," he says.

"How can you tell?" Wyatt asks. Soft-spoken guy, Wyatt, but when you listen you realize that's deceptive. Because he's always talking straight, speaking real thoughts and asking direct questions.

"A lot of reasons. You could see the whole game shifting during the maneuvers, Louisiana and especially Carolina. You could see the big boys waking up, seeing what's been happening in Europe, the difference Tankism is making. Tanks were nothing special, a novelty, up until now. Now they know."

"That doesn't mean we're not the top, though," Logan says. He always sounds like he's in a rush. Like there's something else more important he has to do right after he's finished saying something, even if he just sits there quiet afterward. Then he does it again. Could get irritating, I imagine, but I like him okay now.

"Patton," Cowens snaps. "That's all you need to know. General Patton is commanding the Second Armored Division, so that's all you need to know right there. That's the Tanking genius, that man practically invented the whole business. No, if divisions were bananas, the First would be second, and the Second would be top."

All I can do in this situation is hope that nobody makes any other "bananas" connections regarding our commander. At least not out loud.

"Commander?" Pacifico says.

"Yes?"

There is a certain something here that I have never quite experienced before. We are cooped up in this compact metal machine. It's cold and dark and it's the edge of an island off the edge of a new continent, off the edge of war. And with our disembodied voices floating in this complete foreign *unknown*, I feel unusual. A rush of something comes over me, really strange, not entirely welcome, not entirely bad.

Need. Just like that, I'm welded, like it or not, to these guys, this team, like I have never been to any team before. And there have been a lot of teams.

"Where are we going?" Pacifico asks. "I mean, to fight."

"Fight?" Logan says, rushed, but jokey. "Who said anything about fighting?"

"I came here to fight," I say, not jokey at all.

"Well, I didn't come here to *not* fight," Pacifico says.

"I did," says Wyatt. "I came here to not fight. But I suppose if you guys get into trouble I'll back you up."

"France," Cowens says.

"Yeah?" I say.

"Yeah. Well, I don't know anything for sure, of course. I mean, why would they tell me? If they were gonna tell me stuff like that I'd probably be in the Second, right? But it just makes sense. Look at the map, look at the way the war's going. The Americans are over here now, and we're not here to Mickey Mouse around. I think we are part of a much larger force being assembled for the invasion of France. It's gotta be the invasion of France. We will liberate the French and then storm straight across and into Germany for the big finish."

"Yes!" I say, too loud for the confines, but there was nothing I could do about it.

"Yeah! Yes! Yes! Alllll right! Yeah!"

I think the team's ready for France.

PART TWO
AFRICA

CHAPTER FIVE

For Lost Time

Thank you, Northern Ireland. Thank you for your faith and your moors and peat bog land and your hospitality. Thank you for your stunning, pounding, ancient, and fierce take-no-prisoners rocky coast. Thank you for your challenging hills and rotten, soggy weather and for my first-ever steps off of American soil.

Thank you, *Queen Mary* and Brooklyn, Fort Knox, Fort Jackson, Fort Dix. Thank you, Carolina and Louisiana. Thank you all for getting this fighting force to this point of hardness, readiness, knowledge, stamina, meanness, confidence, anger, and above all, frustration.

Now go away. Dismissed. That'll be it, one and all. We'll take it from here.

Britain's been fighting this thing since 1939 and has gotten more bloody noses out of it than Joe Louis's sparring partners. Allies have already come and gone in the course of it as Germany has snacked on countries big and small all along its wicked path. Even France gave up by 1940. Big ol' France. You look at the map today and you . . . well, you don't want to look at the map.

Then, since the Empire of Japan kindly invited us to the party over ten months ago, our boys have been out in the Pacific Theater, taking on the Japanese — who seem to be having exactly the effect on that part of the world that the Germans are having on this one. Our guys are chasing the Japanese fleet all over that ocean, and engaging their soldiers on hundreds of tiny little islands that nobody ever heard of before but that are right now critical to peace in this world. It's been fierce over there for some time, and the numbers don't sound good. In April we surrendered a place called Bataan that I never even knew we had to begin with. Never knew it existed. I know it now, though, like everybody else. Seventy-six thousand allied soldiers were taken prisoner, twelve thousand of them our boys. Japanese then forced them all on a sixty-mile march to a new camp, no water, no food in the murderous sun. Five thousand fewer American servicemen, that's what we had at the end of that sixty-mile death march in Bataan. Bataan. Has this thing spread so much that they're having to make up new places to contain it all? Bataan is a huge, strategically important, famous place right now. When the war is done with it, will Bataan still be that?

Will Bataan still *be*?

But the thing that has been completely unreal during all the horror has been, frankly, us. We've been there in spirit, on paper, in theory, but not for *real*. An American military presence is so sorely needed in the European Theater of the war. We need to at least show up and stand up straight and make the bully know that it's simply not gonna go all his way just like that anymore. From December 7, 1941, and the bombing, which really made the whole idea of *declaring* war feel kind of absurd, to December 11, when *Germany* officially declared war on *us*, just to make sure everybody got the stupid, stupid joke, and on through February of '42, and April, and October, we have been *officially* engaged in this war, Europe as well as Asia, Germany as well as Japan. Yet the *official* status just floated there alongside the bloody, destructive truth of a war that was being fought, physically, by others. Through all that, not one American unit had been engaged in the European Theater of the war. Hitler's Theater. He held the stage, that's for sure.

Until now. That all changes as of right now, 'cause we're moving out, and the Nazis aren't gonna know what hit 'em.

Hannah and I exchange letters once a week. No matter what day each of our letters arrives in the mail, we have an agreement that neither one opens and reads until Sunday. That way it's more like we are having a conversation together and we're not separated by thousands of miles. I originally wanted to set a time as well, to allow for the difference in time zones and everything, until Hannah pointed out that that may be a little impractical and restrictive. She used different words than that, one of them being *lunatic*, but we understood each other well enough. I always feel like she's reading right when I'm reading, though.

DEAR HANNAH,

WE ARE finally moving, which EVERYbody hERE is PRETTY EXcited About. So AfTER five VERY long months in NoRThERN IRElAND thAt SEEMED liKE five yEARS (nothing PERSONAl, NI) WE ARE dis-pAtching to ... ENglAND. Which, AS I uNdERSTAND it, is PART of thE SAME UNitEd KiNgdom thAt NoRThERN IRElAND belongs to. I AM VERY tiRED, HANNAH, of ENgAging with No onE but AMERicANs ANd Allies EVERY dAy of my ENlisTMENT so fAR with EVERYthing ElSE thAt's going on so bRutAlly everywhere else. I am so worked up and frustrated, I'm like a big pineapple hand grenade on legs walking around and somebody's pulled my pin out. I think maybe to relieve some of the pressure when we travel south from here to England we'll see if we can go out of our way to pick a fight with Scotland to blow off some steam. From what I gather from other Brits I've met, the Scots will be happy to oblige, with very little provocation.

I miss you. I miss home. I miss baseball (please tell me baseball misses me back). Mostly, I think, I miss action. I would like to have a sense that I am doing something, something right and worthwhile, every day when I get up. I am sure once we get to our real destination (I don't know where or when that is, but everybody senses it coming now), all that missing-missing foolishness will subside in a hurry.

Oh. Not you. I didn't mean that. I think about you every day and I know I will no matter how many towns I liberate or battalions I capture single-handedly. (I apologize for being brash and boastful there, but I had to get it out. I just feel like we can't lose. I honestly

feel we will not be defeated, anywhere, by anybody, once they let us in. Is that immodest? If
you feel the need to upbraid me on this, then feel
free to do so. Maybe it's a bad way to sound, but
probably a good way to feel, approaching battle.)

Yours fondly,
Roman Bucyk

Dear Roman,

President Roosevelt has done many fine and noble things since he has been in office, but I think that when he wrote, "I honestly feel that it would be best for the country to keep baseball going," right when some people were saying the game should shut down for the war, that just said a lot about who he is as a man, what he understands about the lives of regular folk. I thought it sounded like something you could have said, and maybe you did. Maybe you could run for president when you're finished over there. You will need a job, after all, and it won't be baseball, since the Red Sox called and signed me up as soon as you left. They even said I had a better arm than you, which I thought was rather flattering. (It is hard not to conclude that they were just waiting for you to be out of the way so they could give me your spot in the organization, don't you think?)

Are you wearing your scapular? Well, of course you are. It's keeping you safe, you know.

I do have some news to report regarding my war effort as well. Unfortunately, my application for the new Women's Auxiliary Ferrying Squadron — WAFS — has been turned down. As it turns out, the commercial pilot's certificate that I had almost completed before I got myself preoccupied with baseball (and certain baseball players) was a firm requirement, as they do not have time to train people below that level and without five hundred hours of flying time already. I am awfully disappointed, to be honest, but they say they had over twenty-five thousand applicants for fewer than two thousand spots. At least it proves the women of America are as ready and willing as you guys are.

There is a consolation, though. I went and signed up for the WAACs — the Women's Army Auxiliary Corps, if you don't know — and got myself assigned to the Army air base at Newcastle, Delaware. Just right up the road, practically. Which just happens to be the base of the very same WAFS. I am going to be a part of this thing, Roman, you just watch me.

I might even make it into the action before you do. (That's supposed to make you laugh, not get you even more frustrated and picking fights with anybody.)

Are you proud of me? I am. Hope you're proud of me. I know you are. The Fighting Bucyks! Here we go.

Love and prayers to you,

Hannah

Of course I am proud of her. Holy cats, am I proud of her, although she does *not* have a better arm than me. In a lot of ways we are still getting to know each other and rather than that being a scary thought, I find it exciting, because every new thing I learn makes me feel even more certain. Certain that this is exactly the person I would have built in my mad scientist laboratory if I wished to produce my ideal and indeed had the powers. As fresh data continues to roll in, I admire it all.

Even stuff like that pilot training, for example. And the application to the WAFS, which is true pioneering business, and brave. And her clever way of writing about it as if I had ever heard one word of it before. Which I hadn't. That could have been an oversight on Hannah's part. But since Hannah doesn't tend to commit anything as sloppy as an oversight, one could conclude otherwise.

The WAFS program, and another called the Women's Flying Training Detachment out of Houston, are great examples of what makes America the best of all possible countries. People coming up with creative ideas to solve desperate problems, whipping up whole new services that never even existed before and then locating the smartest and bravest, most capable people to take on the jobs. We have been desperately low on capable pilots. These programs are going to provide a huge service in training women pilots to fly aircraft from factories to bases and ports, transport cargo, fly simulated missions for training, and even tow targets for antiaircraft artillery practice. Women will fly back home, freeing the men to get into the live action all over the world.

Hannah would be outstanding at that job, no doubt the best, eventually. So the WAFS missed a trick there.

Thank goodness.

I know that doesn't sound right. Hannah's an incredibly able, tough, and talented gal, and, okay, she might even have a better arm than me. I admire this and everything else about her and know she would be absolutely the top flier in our program, never mind theirs, and she is acting the way I want every single American to act about this war.

But I'd rather fight the whole German panzer army by myself, on my bike, with a slingshot, than to think of some novice artillery gunners learning their craft by shooting at a target, towed by a plane, piloted by the person whose very face I see when I look past the war.

And that is why she did not keep me apprised along the way. She feels I have an unhealthy need to control all aspects of every situation. It's not a need. It's just for everyone's best.

So now I just have to worry about what they'll have her doing in the WAACs.

It is cold and raw and as November as November gets when we put out to sea. Who cares? The adrenaline and sense of mission alone are enough to warm every man on board and probably power all the ships as well. We are in a convoy of well over a hundred vessels of all description, mostly British Royal Navy, but some of ours, too. It's a real hodgepodge, as I can see while hanging over the side of our transport ship. It's an LST (Landing Ship, Tank), which is basically a big old cargo ship converted with a massive steel door on its nose that drops down like a drawbridge to deliver men and machinery right onto the beach. From its deck, I look out and take in the details of the rest of our armada. There is one real-deal aircraft carrier and a couple more that look like cargo ships that have had runways stuck on top. There are Coast Guard cutters converted to junior destroyers, troop ships, and what we'd have to call troop ship draftees — commercial ferries fitted for as many soldiers and vehicles as they'll hold. It's whatever it takes at this stage, and it's hard to see it without feeling a kind of motley pride at the effort of it all.

By the end of the first day's sailing, though, it's not hard to remember why we are Army and not Navy men. Pacifico, Wyatt, and myself are spending as much time as we can up on top deck, necks craning, gulping for fresh air. We alternate between here and our makeshift quarters below, which isn't much more than mattresses and blankets thrown on the floor in a bare storage unit.

It's when we come down for the third or fourth time, around sunset, that Commander Cowens gives us the word. Secrecy was so tight we didn't even know our destination when we launched, but now he can give us at least that much.

It is not what we were expecting.

"What?" Wyatt says, well above his normal tone. "Where is *that*?"

Logan, who is standing with Cowens and has clearly already had some time to digest the information, bursts out laughing at Wyatt's shock. He laughs alone, however.

"Algeria," Cowens repeats. "It's in North Africa."

"Oh, swell," Wyatt says, throwing his hands up like he's surrendering already, though I doubt that's what he means. "So now we got a beef with the Algerians and we gotta make a side trip to fight in Africa? This is gonna take forever."

I do almost feel like laughing at this point but can't quite manage it. What I can manage is to drop right down on the closest mattress cross-legged while Cowens gives the class a lesson.

I'm thinking about the map. I'm thinking that we sail right past France, on our way to the Mediterranean, to get to North Africa. The Nazis seem farther away than ever at this moment and I'm sure they have no idea how lucky they are.

"Apparently, the thinking is that we're gonna hit 'em low, come up out of Africa and get to the Germans through Europe's weak spot."

"Italy," Pacifico says, sadly enough that he makes me look up. "Why does everybody forget about the Italians? We're always talking about fighting the Germans, when we're fighting the Italians, too."

Don't know why, but I never made the connection, with Pacifico being Italian and all. But it sure is clear now that he's made the connection, and that it means something to him.

Commander Cowens reaches out and claps Pacifico medium hard, with a *pap* on the neck.

"Don't you worry, I promise you we won't forget the Italians."

That could very easily go a number of ways, most of them not so great. But Cowens hangs onto the kid's neck, shakes him a little, smiles, and Pacifico responds with that goofy grin and we're all right.

"But don't worry about Italy just now. There is a lot of grit and grief between hitting North Africa and even thinking about crossing that warm little sea. Just ask the Brits."

We sort of sleep, mostly don't, do a lot of nervous walking, queasy talking, between decks over the next few days. It's hard to eat much, with the ocean motion causing so much not-quite-digested food to be jettisoned overboard. So I'm getting a bit edgy, anxious, and irritable. I even find myself at one point staring at the ocean like I'm angry with its behavior, so really, things need to turn, soon.

It's a big deal then when we approach the Strait of Gibraltar, and we get to see that famous big rock standing sentry at the remarkably narrow passage between the Atlantic and the Mediterranean. It has been right there, watching over clashes of east and west, north and south, Europe and Africa, for almost as long as people have been warring. And now it's our turn. It's a crossroads if ever there was one, and surely a meaningful checkpoint for this voyage.

"I thought it was just a myth," Wyatt says, admiring it. "Now I seen everything."

"Not even close," Cowens says, laughing. "There's a lot more everything where that came from, young Mr. Why Not."

"Wyatt, sir."

"Yes, why not, indeed. And I suspect you, and we, are going to see more of the world's everything by the time we're done than anybody in history ever saw."

I've got my bearings now. We have slipped around Spain and Portugal, and all I can think is, *we passed right by it.* Somewhere back in that ocean we've been sailing, the coast of France was lying still, all secure, taunting us, watching us make this long curious voyage.

"Thinking of making a sharp, unscheduled left-hand turn back toward northern shores?" Cowens says as I stare out into nowhere that is not nowhere at all. He's right behind me but I don't look back.

"No more than you are," I say.

Truth is, everyone was half expecting we'd be attacked by German U-boats while we were traveling the Atlantic, since they have been savaging Allied convoys. Getting this far unscathed should be cause for not-so-minor celebration. Regardless, we'd both still vote for a U-turn into the U-boats and gamble on our chances.

"We certainly are taking the scenic route to Berlin," he says.

"Certainly are," I say.

"But oh, the sights we'll see," he says as he backs away, patting my shoulder crisply and leaving an eerie reverberation all up and down my whole self.

Then, we pull up. Our convoy stops short of the straits and we make anchor just off Gibraltar. There are already many warships assembled, and throughout the day we watch as more convoys link up, and more, until we have easily well over three hundred vessels.

"Are we *sure* this isn't the invasion of France?" Logan asks as the whole crew of us, along with everybody else aboard, jostles and jockeys for position to see what's unfolding on the sea before us.

"Maybe I was wrong?" Cowens says, surely by accident and surely the only time we will hear him question himself.

"Do I count . . . ten aircraft carriers?" I ask.

"Fifty destroyers?" asks Pacifico.

"Ten cruisers," says Logan, rapidly, getting frustrated with the pacing. "Battleships, minesweepers, antiaircraft ships, submarines . . ."

"Boys," says Cowens, "we're goin' in guns a' blazin'."

There is whooping and barking now all over the place. Just looking at all that hardware makes a guy puff his chest all the way out, like we built it all with our bare hands. I look around, and I see it in everybody, and I have that feeling again: We cannot lose. Ever.

There is a loudspeaker announcement calling us all to assemble on the main deck . . . where pretty much everybody is already assembled. It's an announcement to turn around and listen, basically.

When we do turn we see Captain Dexter, the commanding officer of our ship — which now feels like a big fat rust bucket compared to the flash all around us. He is standing up high on a platform outside the ship's control room, and as he addresses us it's evident he's as eager as we are to get down to business. Once he shares with us what the exact business will be.

"Right, men, so you know that security is paramount and that we have had to be as careful as we could be with the dissemination of information. It's been hard on you, no doubt, being kept in the dark, and your patience has been appreciated. Now it is time for that patience to be rewarded.

"The fleet you see assembled here is going to split into three separate groups, in support of three separate, coordinated assaults along the North African coast. Three aircraft carriers, one battleship, one antiaircraft ship, and nine destroyers will be sailing with us in support of our landings in and around Oran, in Algeria, as the Center Task Force of Operation Torch."

A cheer goes up all around at the very idea that we are a task force of any kind, part of any operation, with a definite objective. Dexter quiets us with his hands up in the air.

"The Eastern Task Force will be led by Lieutenant General Kenneth Anderson and will target Algiers. The Western Task Force will attack at Casablanca under the command of General George S. Patton."

Right behind me I hear a little growl. It is the only such reaction. I'm guessing it's my tank commander.

Captain Dexter has not been distracted. "And if you look just a few hundred yards off our starboard side you will see the *Largs*, which is the headquarters ship for our task force, headed by the commander of Second Corps, Major General Lloyd R. Fredendall."

The low growl behind me takes on some extra thrust, and even forms words.

"Looks like a luxury liner. Patton wouldn't be caught dead on that thing. Typical. The other guys get Old Blood and Guts, and we get Hemorrhoid Lloyd, the sitting-downest, back-seat-drivingest general in the whole show. Probably only lured him here by telling him it was a Mediterranean holiday cruise."

Finally, Cowens's intensity is enough to get me to turn my back on the announcement I've been waiting a year for. I find him, unsurprisingly, scowling.

"Ah, commander," I say, grinning, "don't be such a diplomat. Tell us what you really think of the guy."

He takes that to be a genuine request for more.

"I got some infantry pals who were 'in the field' with him. During maneuvers they knew exactly when they could goof off, because if it rained, or got above eighty-two degrees or below sixty, he refused to come out of his quarters. He phoned in his orders, and *expected his men to follow them.*"

I smile and nod and would laugh if I thought that would be permissible but like a lot of times with Cowens, you just can't be too sure.

Captain Dexter has continued his briefing, probably

more informational but certainly less passionate and entertaining than Cowens's. Now he's concluding.

"To be frank, we are not entirely sure what to expect from the French forces along the African coast. The colonies there are controlled by the French government in Vichy, which means they really take their orders from Berlin. Indications are encouraging that these troops will not offer more than minimal resistance, and the hope is that once we have successfully taken control of the area, these forces may in fact return to the Allied cause. We must, however, be prepared for every eventuality. So, there you have it, men. Get some rest, as we sail in the morning and will be landing in Oran in four days' time. This will be the first American endeavor in the European Theater of Operations. Let's show 'em what they've been missing!"

The roar is full-throated and long-lasting and feels like it might hold right through 'til tomorrow and power the launch all the way to Algeria.

CHAPTER SIX
Torch

But you'll follow orders, right, commander? Even from General Fredendall?"

I must be deranged with the dizzying scent of combat, because I am teasing Commander Cowens as we pick at our gray, leathery food-shapes across the mess table. The five of us are seated and eating like a family for the first time, and it feels right.

"I will follow those orders, no matter how misguided and uninformed, no matter how far those orders have to travel from the source to where the actual fighting is being done. Because I am a good soldier and good soldiers follow even stupid orders. Hey, I'd take orders from General Why Not here if I was required to, and he doesn't even believe Algeria is a real place."

"It's Wyatt," Wyatt says with admirable dignity. "And I believe it now."

Pacifico is really disappointed, almost depressed, over the state of whatever the food is supposed to be.

"I'm kind of insulted by this," he says, looking down gloomily at his plate. He moves stuff around, turning it over, squinting hard at it, like he's desperate to work out a point of entry.

Logan is tearing at his meal as if somebody dared him, or possibly he likes it. "All I know is," he says, chewing vigorously and talking more so, "I *have* to get in that tank and fire that cannon at something right *now*."

"You realize you'll sink us, if you do that *now*," I say.

"I'm afraid, Logan, under those circumstances, I'm going to have to refuse to load," Wyatt says.

Logan seems to be taking this very seriously. Still chewing, but more pensively now, he eventually concedes. "Okay, I'll wait. But not much longer. I ain't kidding."

He's speaking for everybody, although a little more unhinged than the rest. But *not much longer* appears to be upon us, as there is a sudden surge of activity and energy, people rushing out of the mess and up top.

We have finally come within sight of the mystical Oran of our dreams. Cool as you like, we approach it, the whole convoy sailing perpendicular to the coast as if to give them a good long look. It is late in the day on November 7, and the buzz starts crackling through the whole ship and probably the whole convoy. This is it.

We seem to take forever cruising, showing off, sailing eastward like we're not here for a landing at all but just to give them a chance to photograph our good side. Western Task Force is already behind us, having split off shortly after the entire fleet made the harrowing thirty-three hour passage through the Strait of Gibraltar without attracting unfriendly attention. Now we cruise at what feels like slow motion, past Oran, farther past it, as if we are all going to continue on to the Eastern Task Force destination of Algiers.

"They're testing to see if the French coastal defenses have us figured out," Cowens says, "or if they just think we're a supply convoy to the British forces on Malta."

"On what?" Wyatt asks.

I jump in before Cowens can get at him. "How many nicknames are you trying to get?"

"Why What?" Logan says.

"Why Dat?" Even Pacifico is getting in on it.

Before long it is apparent the French think nothing much about our convoy, if they noticed it at all. So we sail on, in the direction of Algiers, well past dark, until it is time to wave off our Eastern Task Force brothers, turn around, and steam for Oran in the dead of night. It is a multinational, Allied operation, but we are learning the politics of it as well. The British are taking on the Algiers landing farther down the coast because of the bad blood that has developed between them and the French over Oran. The Brits bombed the French fleet there to keep it out of German hands, so if we expect any kind of goodwill from French and Algerian forces, this bit needs to have an all-American look. Though the Royal Navy will have us covered discreetly from offshore.

Good thing the French still love the Yanks. I guess.

We are most of the way back after our big U-turn when we hear it. The sound of American and British planes, which departed directly from England, now approaching Oran. The planes are loaded with US paratroopers who are to head straight for the two airfields just outside the town, La Senia and Tafaraoui. The paratroopers will jump there, seize the fields, and neutralize one of the greatest threats to the invasion.

Meanwhile, out way ahead of our convoy, two converted ferries are just about now delivering four companies of rangers to a beach just north of the town of Arzew to slip in and capture the forts and gun batteries that represent the fiercest coastal defense to our Navy.

Our job now is to wait on the rangers. On their signal of objective accomplished, we will storm the beaches.

The planes are passing overhead now, and will reach the fields in a few minutes. The transports have surely placed the rangers, who will be doing what rangers do best, meaning this will be a short wait for us. Which is good because this floating offshore is for the birds.

Suddenly, there is a siren blaring out from the direction of Oran's harbor. Then the lights all go out. We are no secret anymore.

Antiaircraft fire fills the air rat-a-tat rapid, and the sky beyond Oran is popping with explosions. There seems to be more activity inshore than we were expecting. Lots of gunfire snapping from all points along the coast.

Then, it escalates into something more.

Bu-hoom. Bu-hoom. Bu-hoom.

We are under attack, from gun batteries on either side of the town and just beyond it.

All at once, the fighting ships of our flotilla respond, and the artillery fire, from every direction, beside us, behind us, is deafening and creates something like a vacuum of air and sensation in the bubble of our floating world. My ears pop hard, and the diminished hearing is a blessing, then, just as quickly, it's terrifying and I want my senses back. This is what we didn't experience, couldn't experience, in all the maneuvers Carolina could maneuver in a lifetime.

I wasn't expecting this. I wasn't expecting *this*. This is a slugging, back and forth, and I am now noticing the French warships mobilized in the harbor, coming out chin-first and firing large-caliber shells, giving up *nothing* to our superior fleet.

I wasn't expecting this? Was anybody expecting this?

I see our two destroyers now. The two former American Coast Guard ships steaming straight for the enclosed harbor of Oran with the clear intention of undoing any guarding of coasts today. They are bringing in troops to pile right into the heart of Oran, and also to blast that beachfront wide open for the rest of us.

Then, there's an explosion. One of the ships has been hit, the other is rammed by a French destroyer, and it looks like pure dogfight chaos of the kind definitely not advertised to us before now.

I am only a lowly tank driver, but I think things are going wrong.

This, to one degree or another, goes on all night long. I remain poised, frozen in my readiness like a simple devoted dog sure that his master's going to open that door any second. Literally, for hours I hold this status. Already scuttlebutt is circulating about Allied casualties, about at least one ship sunk, about the grand plan not going to plan. But through it all I remain that dog, poised, waiting while the fierceness of the battle seems to lessen, while the explosions and responses come further apart.

Then, a brilliant set of green fireworks flares, dazzling the sky above Algeria. Seconds later, the loudspeaker is blaring at us.

"Report to stations. All personnel, prepare and report to designated stations, ready for assault landing."

From there, it is not even a blur. A guy would have to see some kind of streaky figures, motions, colors in the air to qualify as a blur but there is nothing, not a trace of visual memory as I sit at the controls of my tank, my heart beating like a Spitfire engine in full flight. The crew are all in place as our tank sits still, deep within the hold of the transport. The ship lurches and then powers, steaming straight in toward the Algerian shore as if it's our intention to plow right through it and keep on going.

My division, the First Armored, and the First Infantry Division are landing on three beaches, two to the west of the city and one to the east. Our concern is not really the beaches but those two airfields beyond, where we are supposed to follow up the first wave of troops who landed there and provide that special brand of tank-and-infantry security that means once the Army takes a field, it stays taken.

I've gotten accustomed to the idea that I'm going the long way to the goal I've been chasing for a long time. Taking on the Nazis is what matters. Fighting beats waiting. So we're attacking Algeria, which is occupied by France, which is occupied by Germany, but if that's how we have to get at 'em, then so be it.

My group is deployed to Arzew, to the east of Oran. We are chugging as if there is no end in sight when we start to feel the scrapings of sea bottom below us.

Close to shore, we hit sand earlier than predicted, and the ship bucks, then rights and continues until we hit another.

"What's that?" Pacifico says in a voice that's straining to be calm but is still a little higher than normal. Every one of the thousands of guys we're about to spew onto Oran's beaches is nervous, I guarantee it. Some are just hiding it better than others.

"Feels like we're running aground," I say, like that's no big deal.

"That shouldn't be happening, should it?" he asks me.

"Well, Pacifico, since this is a landing ship, designed to land, and we are on that ship in order to land . . . it should be happening sometime."

We are able to have this little conversation because despite the hugeness of the European Theater of Operations, of II Corps and First Armored Division, Combat Command B (CCB), aboard this massive LST among the flotilla of the Center Task Force of the North African Invasion, Pacifico and I are seated together in the intimate confines of the lower level of the M-4 Sherman tank. As driver, I am set low on the left side of the main compartment while he is just on the other side of the drive train in the assistant driver/machine gunner spot. We can't see much of the outside world as we wait to unload into it.

Bu-hoom!

We can certainly hear and feel the outside world, however, as a serious shell explosion happens right nearby, rocking our craft. The LST is perfect for this, being flat-bottomed, stable, and able to creep well into shore, but that was an unsettling shock all the same. These may be the last barks of the defending forces, but they are attention getters.

"Commander?" I call up to the turret basket where the commander, main gunner, and loader all have their stations.

"Not to worry," Commander Cowens calls down. "We expected token resistance from French forces along the coast. They have no desire to engage Allied forces, if I understand the situation as it was explained to us, so they won't give us any real trouble. It's all leading to where we get to shoot and blow things up, so just stay focused and don't panic."

The French forces. I don't like to admit to being dumbfounded by the big issues we should probably understand. But I have to admit I have still not worked these guys out. How do you fight for your conquerors?

Bu-hoom!

Right, well we might not be panicking, but I can sense in the cozy living space we are in that everybody's a little thrown by what we're experiencing right now. That was another no-fooling blast from the French, casting more than reasonable doubt on the idea that they have no interest in engaging Allied forces.

The commander has already used up all of his very limited patience and tact for this situation.

"Hey!" he bellows up through the hatch right above his head, and I have no doubt at all that the French can hear him. "If you put this much effort into 1940, none of us would have to be here now!"

I believe Commander Cowens does not have the same level of confusion that I have about the French participation in the war.

Then all at once, like a twenty-one gun salute and then some, the big guns on our companion Royal Navy ships fire one more coordinated volley into the shore, with a vengeance. The air is filled with crackle and boom. Then, the additional sound of a full tanker of tank engines growling to life signals that we are about to hit the shore.

The LST grounds for good, and the great slab of steel that is the bay door groans open and slaps the water like a whale's tail.

One by one the tanks roll down the ramp, splashing into the shallow water, and up the beach. We are way back in the line, with the M-3 light tanks hauling out first. They are the arrowhead of a flying column of tanks that will run from Arzew, along the road looping south around Oran to the Tafaraoui airfield.

We can't keep up with the pace of the M-3s, but we do our best to minimize the gap between them and us. As I work the steering levers, jamming forward for speed, I can hardly contain my excitement. When we crash nose-down into the water, bounce, and hurtle up and onto the sand, it's all I can do to keep my wits from the thrill. I am already replaying that bust-out splash vision in my head, and already having to remind myself to stop being a kid, *right now*.

My tank company moves as a unit straight toward the road, with enemy fire still nestled into the northeast about two football fields from where we make land. It's pretty close fighting already, and I'm pretty sure I could hit a baseball farther than they're shooting at us from.

I learn quickly that action makes Pacifico talkative.

"I thought the French were with the Allies," he shouts over the sound of the tank's excited engine, Logan's excited howling, and the commander's commanding everybody to just simmer down and let cool heads prevail.

"They were," I say. "Then they got beat, surrendered to the Germans."

"And what, they joined the other side?"

"Well, yeah. Some of 'em, anyway."

"Aw, how are we supposed to keep up with this?"

"Tell you what, just shoot straight ahead. If you just shoot where I point the tank, and shoot at whoever's shooting at us, you'll do okay."

"I can do that," he yells like somehow I've set him free.

"Yes, you can," I yell back, and follow my nose and my Tankist brethren as directly as I can into the teeth of the war.

That's the deal with conflict, right? Shoot at the shooters, shoot at the shots. All parties understand that, so let's go at it.

Boooom!

The tank rocks, fighting me as I keep on course, and I can see through my slit as our air cover comes swooping in above us. A shell blasts a plume of sand and rock and metal and pieces of what could be con- fused French fighters twenty-five feet up in the air over where that enemy gun battery once was.

From there, it quiets down considerably. Planes are still buzzing about. We hear artillery, but it's infrequent now, and distant. The line of tanks is spread a bit but still tooling along this relatively simple stretch of road at a decent clip on the way to our destination, like a Sunday drive, only a little bumpy and with five pals piled into the car.

"We did it," Pacifico says, looking toward me and sounding both cautious and surprised.

"I think we did," I reply, paying close attention to the road I have never seen before. Through my narrow scope of vision I can already see this place, Oran, Algeria, Africa, as a different place from what I've ever known. Resort-quality beach becomes industrial center with great big fuel tanks lining the roads and gun batteries guarding them from gentle rises that surround the port. Fleeting glances count as sightseeing, but all the architecture looks to me like it's made of white stone something, like the sand of the very beach we just stormed. Then that falls away to reveal palm trees popping up tall out of chalky earth and then flat empty road leading out to the Algerian heartland, whatever that might be.

"Well, all *right*!" Logan whoops. "Mission accomplished. We have *invaded*, boys."

"We haven't done anything," Cowens says. "Keep your wits about you."

"But look, commander," Wyatt says. "There's the airfield. You can see it, just about a half-mile up. It's ours."

Logan whoops again, louder. "There it is," he says.

Pacifico gets all carried away now, excited, but unable to see that far ahead from our lower vantage point. He shoves open the hatch right above his position to get a better look.

"Shut that thing, *now!*" Cowens hollers a fraction of a second before it all kicks off.

The planes that we had stopped paying attention to have come to pay attention to us. And they are not friendlies.

The shell of our tank starts *ratatatatat* pinging with machine-gun fire as first one then another then another plane swoops low on a strafing run. There is a sudden massive explosion probably five lengths up in the line as they begin dive-bombing us.

"Did you hear that?" Pacifico says. "Shot went right off my lid, right after I closed it. I'd have been a goner." He sounds more wide-eyed amazed than worried or thankful or any of those things he probably should be.

"Pacifico!" Cowens shouts. "Coming toward you at two o'clock. Fire that gun, boy!"

Fire, the boy does. Then the turret swings violently around, Wyatt jams a 75-mm shell into the gun, and Logan rocks us all as he fires the boom cannon.

Commander Cowens keeps barking coordinates and instructions, our gunners keep gunning, and I keep driving, guiding us toward the airfield. The French fighter planes are tenacious, going at us like this is the last battle at the end of the world, and I realize they have been scrambled from Tafaraoui itself to make their last stand to hold it. As the battle goes on, we have to slow down some to properly engage them, causing us to take a lot more machine-gun fire and narrowly miss a couple of bombs. I hear one plane, then another take serious hits and then go into that whiny death scream before crashing in two big fireballs just off to the left of the approach road.

We stop completely to stand and fight just as we are about to reach the airfield. Antiaircraft guns from the base's own artillery begin firing on us. All thirty or so of our tanks go all-in, machine gunners absolutely filling the sky with bullets like a plague of exploding locusts and our big guns training on the battery of anti-aircraft. Planes start coming down rapidly now, crashing and ditching all over the area, until the threat is no threat anymore.

It's close to an hour since we splashed ashore, as the tanks gear up and charge straight across that field, directly into the face of those guns, which become less and less effective the closer we get because they are set to aim at the sky and by the time we are halfway across the field we just lay down a line of fire that pummels and finally eradicates the whole battery.

And then, we return to quiet once more.

We sit there in the middle of the field, looking at the smoldering battlements, crashed planes here and there, and listen as another wave of planes approaches from our rear.

"Here we go again?" I say.

"No," Cowens says, boldly flipping up his hatch and looking back. "They're ours. Spitfires, American, British, coming to take up residence on their new airfield."

"*Now* can we say we did something?" Logan asks.

"I suppose," Cowens says, louder now to compete with the Spitfires overhead. "Not much of something, but something."

"Arggghh," everyone chimes in, a mass, jokey groan.

"Children," Cowens says. "I'm surrounded by a big can of kids, who know nothing but will learn soon enough."

We find some space in one of the empty administration buildings, settle in, and hunker down for the night. Despite the sound of battles still going on in other sectors, ships still sending and receiving heavy fire, machine-gun and artillery bursts in the distance, we get pretty comfortable, pretty quick.

I know I do, anyway. I sleep like a hibernating bear straight through until I get pulled back to reality.

"Up, boys, up!" Cowens says, running along the line of bears sleeping on the floor, kicking feet as he goes.

"What?" I say, jumping up from a dead sleep and into my boots.

"Duty calls. We've got a sighting of a column of French Foreign Legion tanks heading right our way, looking for a fight."

"What a coincidence," Logan says. "We just happen to have one for 'em."

Whatever tired we felt has vaporized as the whole crew of us, as well as bunches of other crews, start running like firemen answering an alarm. We barrel out of that building and man our machines.

"You boys just might get educated quickly after all," Cowens says.

"Maybe we'll be the ones doing the educating," Logan says. Logan's lack of confidence seems not to be one of our weaknesses.

We rumble south down the same road the Legionnaires are taking north, and in my head I'm picturing two of those bighorn sheep from the Rocky Mountains running headlong at each other from a great distance to smash skulls so hard the echo bounces around for days.

It isn't quite like that, though, as about forty minutes out, we see them. They have had time to settle in, take cover in hills, and pull on camouflage to wait on us.

We've come with three platoons, a total of fifteen tanks, and they look to have roughly the same number, though with the camo we can't tell for sure.

Commander Cowens is on the radio with other TCs, as well as the platoon leaders, formulating something. We are the number two tank in our platoon, meaning even if it was just our platoon, it wouldn't be Cowens calling the shots. And with this many commanders and commander-commanders lined up it seems to me that a decision could be a long time coming.

But it's quick.

"Bucyk," Cowens shouts, "pull right, in formation with the rest of our group. I want you to stay right on the shoulder of the first tank, and the third will be back on your hip, and so on down the line. Our platoon'll be going right flank, while the center platoon lays down a low line of fire and the third group forms left flank. Got it?"

"Yes, sir!" I say and fall right in alongside the number one tank.

"I trust you other children know what to do?"

"Yes, sir!" Pacifico, Wyatt, and Logan all respond, and I find myself chiming back in, too, even if he wasn't talking to me. Seems I like shouting *Yes, sir!* under highly charged circumstances.

"All right, we're rolling. Go, go, go!"

So, we go. And go and go and go.

Bu-hoom, bu-hoom, hu-hoom! The cannons of all our tanks and all their tanks explode into action at the same time, shaking the whole earth with the thunder of it. There are about five hundred yards of level field between us and the Foreign Legion tanks up on their short hills, but this is a flat-out slugfest. Our center group is doing a great job of peppering their middle while we come in at their flanks, diffusing their attention. I can see out of my peripheral vision that Pacifico is right up out of his seat, practically attacking his machine gun to attack the enemy harder. I hear Wyatt actually making grunting, growling, and barking noises as he pounds one shell after another into the gun just as fast as Logan can launch them. Which is very fast.

At one point I hear a truly strange sound.

"What are we doing?" Cowens asks nobody, since he surely wouldn't be asking any of us. "This is reckless."

Logan and Wyatt apparently find that thought thrilling, as they both let out war whoops, the kind real Indians never make.

Then, we're hit.

It's a shocker. Everybody stops doing their jobs. Except Cowens, of course. I even let my hands go off the levers for a second, nearly stalling our forward progress in the process.

"Fire!" Cowens shouts. "Drive! Do your jobs! Never stop. Never! No matter what!"

The shell that hit us smacked somewhere along the side of the turret, right above and behind me. It rang loud, bounced us a little sideways, but caromed right off.

We are closing in on them, maybe a hundred and fifty yards away.

"I got him now," Logan says, and no sooner has he said it then, *BAM, WHOOSH!*

The tank in the trees right in my line of vision takes the wrath of Logan directly, explodes spectacularly. I watch, even as I drive straight for them, as somebody struggles up out of the top hatch, in flames, and throws himself over the side. The driver's hatch opens, and a flaming tank crewman, a driver like me, makes it halfway through the hatch and then just sort of flops over in the middle, never making it out past his hips. He lies there, half-in, half-out, all burning away. Nobody else comes out.

In succession, *boom-boom-boom-boom*, the tanks lined up against us on the right get hit and go up, like some giant, lethal carnival shoot-'em-up game.

Another shell scores a direct hit on us, this time smack on the armor plating in front of me. And again it deflects away without doing much.

It's obvious now, and inevitable. The French Foreign Legion is making no motion to surrender, and the tanks of the US First Armored Division are making no motion to give them a chance.

It's a slaughter. We eradicate their entire force.

There is already wild celebrating going on within our tank, and we can hear it all up and down the line. This is an unqualified success, as well as being our first real, true, proper battle to the death, and we came out on top, way on top.

The rush is incredible. Good and bad.

We did exactly what we were supposed to do, as well as we could have done it.

I already know I will never forget the sight of that driver burning away right in front of us. Or the guys we didn't see, inside.

It was brutal.

It was also right.

Commander Cowens is more subdued than the rest of us during the triumphant trip back to Tafaraoui. He doesn't shut us up, but he doesn't join in.

He doesn't say anything until we are passing into the grounds of the airfield itself, now looking as American as Fort Dix, with all the aircraft and troops and whatnot setting up and making it home.

As the tank rolls to a stop and we shut down, he says, almost sadly, "Enjoy this, fellas. Really do, for now. But know this: that if those poor no-quit Foreign Legion fools out there weren't sent in World War One tanks, with World War One ordnance, we wouldn't be here right now to be celebrating anything."

The celebration goes down several notches.

"You all did fine, I'm not criticizing you guys. But if we, all of us, don't fight smarter, more tactically clever than we did today, we are in trouble. I promise you the Germans, Field Marshal Rommel and his panzers, will surely show us how it's done."

There is a short, respectful silence, which is naturally broken by Logan.

"Bring 'em on, sir."

Cowens laughs ruefully, shakes his head, and pulls himself up through the hatch and out.

The other four of us, the *kids*, hang back, sitting in the M-4 Sherman, *our* tank. We look back and forth, one to another, and we start nodding, nodding.

We all feel it. Bring 'em on.

We cannot be beaten.

CHAPTER SEVEN
The Road to Tunisia

DEAR HANNAH,

WHAT HAVE YOU BEEN UP TO? ME, I CONQUERED A COUNTRY. ALGERIA. ACTUALLY, YOU COULD SAY I CONQUERED AN ENTIRE REGION. NORTH AFRICA.

OKAY, YOU'VE PROBABLY GATHERED THAT I HAD SOME HELPERS. THERE WERE ABOUT A HUNDRED THOUSAND OF THEM, TO BE HONEST, BUT THINGS MOVED PRETTY FAST, SO I DIDN'T GET TO MEET A WHOLE LOT OF THEM. WONDERFUL GUYS, I'M SURE.

THERE ARE FOUR, THOUGH, THAT I WISH I COULD INTRODUCE YOU TO. MAYBE THAT CAN HAPPEN, WHEN THIS JOB IS FINALLY ALL DONE, AND DONE RIGHT. I'D LIKE THAT. THESE CAN BE THE FIRST PEOPLE WE HAVE OVER, WHEN WE HAVE OUR PLACE AND EVERYTHING. NICE TO THINK ABOUT, HUH?

UNLESS THEY'RE A BUNCH OF JERKS, OF COURSE. BUT THEY'RE NOT. IN THE TANK'S SETUP WE'RE THREE UP (IN THE TURRET) AND TWO DOWN. I'M THE DRIVER, of course, and next to me in what you might call the copilot seat is a guy named Pacifico. He's both my assistant and machine gunner. He's an awfully good kid, and maybe a little sensitive for this business but I'm pretty sure he's going to toughen up real quick over the next few weeks and months. Upstairs is the gunner, Logan, who works the big cannon. Now, when we have these guys to dinner you might want to seat Logan at the far end of the table because he can be a little excitable. But he's just a big cowboy kid, really, and I'm glad we have him. Wyatt is the guy who keeps the guns loaded, especially Logan's, because we don't want Logan getting bored and looking for something to do. Wyatt's a strange guy. He's a draftee like Pacifico, only he seems a lot less informed about what we are involved in and, usually, where we even are. He doesn't mind asking, though, which is helpful for him and a lot of fun for the rest of us.

But the biggest truth of it all is that we're a bunch of Army kindergartners. We are a crew that lacks experience in a division that lacks experience, and the man who makes everything work is our tank commander. His name is Cowens,

AND HE'S A HARD MAN. HE CAN BE VERY HARD TO FIG-
URE OUT FROM ONE MINUTE TO THE NEXT BUT I
WORKED OUT THAT THE MOST SUCCESSFUL APPROACH IS
TO NOT TRY TO FIGURE HIM OUT. ONCE I WORKED
THAT PART OUT, THINGS MADE A LOT MORE SENSE.
I WILL SAY THIS, THOUGH. CAN'T THINK OF ANYONE I
HAVE PERSONALLY RESPECTED MORE. I WOULDN'T TELL
ANYBODY ELSE BECAUSE I DON'T WANT TO SOUND ALL
GUSHY, BUT WHILE COMMANDER COWENS IS NO JIM
THORPE, HE'S ABOUT AS CLOSE AS A NORMAL PERSON
COULD BE.

I'D APPRECIATE IT IF YOU DIDN'T REPEAT THAT
WHEN THEY COME TO DINNER, AS THE GUYS WOULD RAG
ME SOMETHING AWFUL.

AND JUST THINK, DESPITE HOW GREEN WE MOSTLY
ARE, WE ARE WINNING, HANNAH. WINNING BIG. WE'RE
ONLY GOING TO GET STRONGER FROM HERE, AND I
BELIEVE WE WILL BE HAVING THAT DINNER A LOT SOONER
THAN YOU EXPECT.

WE ARE ON THE MOVE AGAIN RIGHT NOW, REALLY
FLYING, ON TO THE NEXT BIG THING, SO I HAVE TO CUT
OFF HERE.

BUT, I JUST WANT TO SAY SOMETHING. EVERY TIME
I DO SOMETHING, SOMETHING NEW, AND DIFFICULT,

114

something strong and right, my first thought is I can't wait to tell Hannah.

Dopey, huh? Like a little kid with a good report card, huh?

Until next report.

Your dope,
Roman

Dearest Roman,

Did you hear? I don't know how it works over there but I imagine it must be chaotic trying to get information with everything going on. I'm sorry if you've already heard this. Actually, I'm sorry if you haven't. Bill Thomas, who played with you on the Centreville Sox. He hit .270 that last year, remember? He joined the Army Air Corps, like a lot of folks around here signed up after that last game, after you and Nardini and the rest were called out by the mayor, for the crowd to cheer, and with the band and everything. I'm sorry. I just heard that Bill Thomas was killed. He was a pilot in the Air Corps, like Ted Williams. Bill's plane was shot down in North Africa. I'm sorry.

Roman, you told me that if I felt the need, that I should feel free to tell you if I feel you are being too boastful so I am going to take you up on that right now. You have to stop. It's scaring me. You cannot say that you cannot lose, because you can. You can lose, as fine a soldier as you are, you can lose. We all can. I'm scared.

I can't write any more now. I had more to tell you, but it will have to wait. I'm sorry about that. I'm sorry for Bill, and I'm sorry for scolding, and I'm sorry for saying I'm sorry so much.

It's all right for you to be confident, but it's not all right for you to be stupid.

I'm not calling you stupid but if that's how it sounded I'm sorry for that, too.

But don't say it anymore. Please.

Love,

Hannah

"Hellooo," the voice calls, loud enough, but calls again when I don't respond. It may be the third or fourth time because I'm only now becoming aware that I was already hearing it. I'm finally brought completely around to what's happening by a wild knocking on my helmet.

I turn to find that the helmet-knocking was coming from above, where Logan was reaching down with the butt of his pistol and rapping hard enough to make a decent ringing sound. The hello was coming from Pacifico, who was trying to inform me that the column was about to start up again and his shift at driving was over.

"Right," I say, "right." I tuck the letter back into my pocket and we climb over-under to take our proper assignments and start moving down the road once more.

"You okay, kid?" Cowens calls down as I ease the levers ahead into the long column of tanks.

"I am, sir, thanks."

"Good," he says. "It'd be a shame after all this to get knocked out of commission because our driver got distracted and ran us straight into a boulder or off a cliff."

"I don't see any cliffs, commander," Wyatt says, and already I am happy for the diversion Wyatt is bringing. "Are there cliffs where we're going?"

"Argghh," Logan groans, and everybody but me starts laughing in a here-we-go-again fashion.

I'll laugh soon. Very soon. Just not right this minute.

It is certainly no mistake that we drive slowly and deliberately through small towns and villages as we set off for Tunisia. This is a show of strength, a statement of seriousness, and, frankly, a big dog growling over a smaller dog as we motor down the main roads of scenic little coastal spots. The sun is shining, and I can't quite believe the variety I see. Christian cathedrals tower over sidewalk cafés and modern office buildings that would not be out of place in Boston. But in the same blocks, we see mosques and bazaars that are straight out of some Aladdin movie to my eyes. Skinny dogs seem to roam at will, and the folks on the sidewalks are in suits and ties, looking quite French, or in Arab robes and looking a million degrees different. We are allowed to be looking out our individual hatches, and I find myself thinking, holy cow, what a great vacation this must have been.

I hear French and Spanish and some English and some languages I couldn't dare guess at, and it feels like another world for sure. Pacifico waves, at nobody specific, which is good because nobody waves back, specifically or generally.

And I realize, there is no joy for us here. Whatever side they are on today or were on yesterday, nobody on these streets is particularly happy to see our tanks crunching through their hometowns.

"You're welcome, and good riddance," Logan says, slamming his hatch shut as we exit a town and hit open road. "Enjoy going back to being a great big no-place in the world there, Algeria."

"No place is ever no-place," Cowens says sternly. "Algeria's important to the world now, as it was before, as it will be again. Read your history, kid, and learn something."

"What do you know about Tunisia, commander?" Pacifico calls up when we have been following the column into ever more barren flatlands for ages.

There is a pause.

"Well, it's over . . . there someplace. I think."

I catch a quick glimpse up over my shoulder to see him pointing. Very straight-arm, land-ho like. He gives me a wink and I turn my gaze back in the direction of actual Tunisia.

We are somewhere in the middle of the pack of what looks to me like the kind of awe-inspiring tank column that would intimidate me out of my wits if I saw it thundering my way. Within only a few days of securing all of our objectives in Algeria and Morocco, Combat Command B has been sicced like a big bad dog on the Axis forces in Tunisia, with the balance of II Corps right behind us.

I promise you, Hannah, I won't say it anymore.

But I feel it. I feel it right this minute, and there's nothing I can do about that.

There's nothing that I *want* to do about that.

"So let me see if I got this straight," Wyatt says, and

bless him, he sounds like he's trying. "What we just accomplished back there, means that the French Army and Navy, they've surrendered to us."

Cowens sounds very pleased. "Not exactly," he says with a laugh in his voice like one of those wise guy history teachers from high school.

"Then *what* exactly?" says Wyatt.

"Why Not, exactly," calls Logan, in a pretty good Wyatt voice.

"Shut *up*, exactly," Wyatt shouts. "At least I'm making an effort to understand what's going on."

"Man's got a point," Pacifico calls out.

"He does, too," Commander Cowens says. "The kid is giving it his all. Say, I know. Why don't we let you explain it to him, Logan?"

And that's why he's the boss man.

We all wait. Then we stop waiting.

"Bwaa-haaa-haaa . . . !"

I'm betting we're making enough noise that the vehicles in front and behind are straining to see what all the fun's about.

"Hey, I understand it," Logan says, a little quieter and a lot less convincingly than he says most things. "I just don't know how to explain it so that he'll understand it."

The boss drops a dubious "Uh-huh," like a very small bomb on Logan's explanation, then moves on to something a little more helpful.

"The forces of French North Africa have agreed to an armistice with the Allies."

Now, the configuration — of this tank, I mean, not the many nations involved in this conflict — is set up so that Wyatt is sort of in the spot above and behind me. So right now I am missing what is probably a pretty good visual. The audio helps me to get a decent mental picture of poor Wyatt's expression of concentration.

"C'mon, kid, I know you can do it," Cowens says, almost sweet. For Cowens.

"The French are back on our side, then!" Wyatt says happily.

"Some of them are!" Cowens says just as happily.

"Which ones?"

"Well, the Resistance fighters, the Free French, were always with us."

"So who wasn't?"

"The Vichy French."

There is a silence that indicates a little more suspicion than usual from Wyatt. It seems he trusts the downstairs crew more not to pull his leg.

"Pacifico?" he says. "Is this real?"

"I think so, Wyatt. Bucyk?"

It's the most fun we're likely to have for a while, so I don't see any need to cut it unnecessarily short. "Is what real, Wyatt?"

"Vichy French. I mean, of course I heard it before, but I just thought it was some kind of insult, like, oh that dirty rat, he's a real Vichy French. . . ."

There is a physical commotion upstairs that is unsettling enough that I think a fight might have broken out.

"Cut it out, Logan," Wyatt protests loudly. "I do not like to be kissed. Captain!"

The scrambling is ended by Cowens apparently heaving Logan back into his seat.

"No kissing in my tank," Cowens says. "And anyway, he was right. *Vichy French* is an insult. Kid knows more about world events than the rest of you put together."

"Don't ever change, Wyatt," Logan says.

"If you don't want me to change then I'm pretty sure I better start changing as fast as I can."

"All right," Cowens says, "playtime's over. The situation is this. When the Germans whipped the French, they occupied the north of the country directly. They left the south — and the French colonies in North Africa — to supposedly govern themselves, from Vichy in the south of France. It was a puppet government, French in name but run by Germany, which became plenty obvious when we won in Algeria and Morocco and the troops there turned. As soon as that happened, Germany decided that was enough, and just swept all the way down. Now all of mainland France is German. That's where that stands."

"So what does that mean?" Pacifico asks.

I take the liberty.

"It just means the Nazis are that much closer to where we can get our hands on 'em," I say.

I've impressed the boss.

"I like your optimism, Bucyk," he says. "Truth is, they're a lot closer than that. The Brits have been rallying lately, driving them out of Egypt and Libya, sending them retreating right this way."

"We've got a date," I say.

"With the real German Army this time. With Rommel himself."

"Come to papa," Logan growls.

"So there are no more French troops in Tunisia?" Pacifico asks.

"There are. But they just did a crisp about-face. They're fighting *against* the Germans, who are going to be pretty surprised."

"For once I understand how the Germans feel," says Wyatt.

For a good week, it feels like we're on a well-earned post-invasion holiday as we cruise along in our great steel line across vast uncontested stretches of road. As far as we can see, the farther inland one gets in North Africa, the drier and flatter it gets. There always seems to be something on the horizon, *over there*, and *over there*: cobalt blue sea, gentle hills, high plateaus. But you never get there. It's always away, off someplace, while *right here* is always sand and rocks and boulders and rocks and sand, and the taste of dust is relentless. Dust in the mouth, the eyes, the gears of everything. But it's quiet, anyway, which is okay.

"This is going to be easy," Logan proclaims, breaking a long period when the tank's engine did all the talking.

The statement seems to have gotten right up Commander Cowens's nose.

"You do realize, don't you, Logan, that merely driving across however many miles of country is not the same as actually *taking* those miles of country, do you not?"

It's a tone of voice even Logan doesn't dare to play with.

"Yes, sir, I do."

"Good. Then, keep your wits. The easiest thing in the world is to let your senses go flat during a mundane stretch like this, and that is when you will make crucial errors of judgment or execution."

"Yes, sir, commander. I'll keep an eye on my wits, sir."

Now, there he's coming dangerously close to playing with him. Probably out of the very boredom the commander is addressing.

Suddenly, there's a something. It's a small something at first but I notice it just as I notice Pacifico noticing it, the way dogs do that rigid-alert posture when there's a bumblebee somewhere just outside of human hearing range and just inside of dog hearing range.

Only then, and quick, it comes within everybody's range.

The road we are taking runs southeast, into the heart of Tunisia, and the planes are coming at us from the north. Not flying straight into our faces, but obvious enough to be pretty bold. We can see them coming for miles, and hear them from even farther, and it's strange, surreal, the way it feels like there is nothing else in this vast and spare landscape other than our tanks and their aircraft. It is a world devoid of anything other than warfare. At the same time, it doesn't feel, for the first little while, like anything particularly hostile is happening.

Then they get closer. Faster, closer, faster, louder, closer.

The sound is wild, wicked, like nothing I've ever experienced. The formation, maybe a couple dozen planes, fans out shortly before they reach us so that the front of our column and us in the middle of the pack receive the same greeting at the same time.

"Guns up, gentlemen!" Cowens yells, and we start firing at the same time the planes do.

I keep driving, jamming both levers full forward to keep up with the accelerating convoy, as the machine-gun rounds and antiaircraft shells pop all over the sky, making a great racket and smoke.

But our racket is nothing compared to theirs.

Dive-bombers swoop insanely low, dropping a load and banking back up as the explosion below seems to boost them faster into the sky.

We are strafed mercilessly by pilots who I swear look me straight in the face as they bear right down on us. You can feel the *whoosh* of their slipstream as they skim right over our heads.

But the sound. There is a type of plane in the mix that screams, a haunting, intimidating screech that would probably do enough damage if they showed up and harassed us with no explosives at all.

"Commander, what is *that*?" I scream, nowhere near above the din, but enough to reach the boss.

"It's a Stuka," he shouts back. "The devil's own bomber. They got sirens or some such attached. Been terrorizing everybody everywhere with those things, since even before the war started."

"Aw," Logan says, taking aim at one, "and I thought we were special."

He lets fly, *bu-hoom*, misses, and I am certain I can hear the plane laughing as it departs.

"I can't stand it," Wyatt screams.

"It's just a trick," Cowens assures him, "a gimmick. Keep loading, kid."

"It's a *great* trick," he says, jamming a seventy-five up the cannon, "a *great* gimmick. Fire, Logan!"

Logan fires, and it feels as if we are making noise as much for the noise as to shoot anything down.

Next to me, firing away but saying nothing, my gunner Pacifico is making a strange noise of his own. It starts medium-loud, medium-high, but quickly builds both strength and pitch until it's a pretty eerie thing all its own.

Finally, he hits his note.

It's an exact copy of the Stuka sound.

I glance over at him, and he is as grim as death's sensitive little brother. There isn't even a sign that he's aware he's doing it, but he is doing it, so relentlessly I don't know how his lungs are managing to refuel.

They are rolling in, bearing down on us again, this formation of four, two of the ugly gull-wing Stukas and two of the ME-109 fighters that we had seen before at Oran. Several of the other fighter-bomber groups have already peeled off back in the direction they came from, but I guess in the end we are special because these four are coming down like they intend to just dive straight into us without stopping.

They don't, of course. The first Stuka drops a bomb that lands close off to our left and makes our tank do a little hop, while both fighters pepper us with a diabolical barrage of machine-gun fire that has us all hollering wordless yelps into the air. The bullets make the Sherman sound like a tin can filled with rocks and shaken up wildly by some mad giant.

The second Stuka pilot is bold or stupid or confused or something because he holds his load longer than the rest, trailing in after the others have already banked.

The sound is demented, dementing all of us with it.

Pacifico screams louder, its exact song right back at it, and stares straight into it as he murders the rounds right out of his .30, pushing them with his will up and out, and in . . . right into the side and the wing and then the retreating tail of that bomber before it can do its dirty business at all.

We are all screaming as we stare at that aircraft limping away, off-level and trailing delicious German oil smoke across the sky in pursuit of its rotten friends.

Its payload drops off like an accident, a turd off a bird, and pops harmlessly in the desert beyond where anybody cares about what happens.

Then it's over. It's just us again, our line of tanks in the sand. Alone with our thoughts.

And the screaming in our ears that remains as a gift from above.

"*Great* shooting there, kid," Cowens says, hanging down from the turret basket to reach in and slap Pacifico hard on the shoulder. Wyatt does likewise while a slightly frustrated-sounding Logan shouts out congratulations from his station. He could well be waiting for a straggler and another chance to gun somebody down.

"Really," I say to Pacifico, leaning sideways toward him while still driving forward toward the enemy. "Fine work, pal."

I shift back to where I belong when I hear the barely smiling machine-gunner still humming that eerie tune.

"By the way," Commander Cowens says, "I completely forgot my manners. Rookies, meet the German Air Force, the Luftwaffe. Luftwaffe, these are my rookies."

"Nice to meet you," Logan says, speaking for the team.

"Commander," I say because this seems like the perfect time, "you seem to be pretty well acquainted with these guys."

"Oh yes, we're old pals. We go way back."

"But since we've only been in the war less than a year, and we only just landed in-theater about . . ."

"Young Bucyk, I was trading punches with these guys when you were still in short pants. Civil War in Spain. Franco's Fascists, Hitler's Nazis, and me. Everybody who was anybody was there. That was before I was even getting paid. That's what a dumb kid I was."

He may have a long and colorful tale to tell about that, but I wouldn't be surprised if he cut it off right there. Then his radio cuts it off for him.

I'm starting to think it might be something more than a love of tanks that fuels the boss's engine.

There is a whole lot of phone chatter for the next couple of hours, between our commander and probably a number of different levels of commanders on the other end of the line. He's pretty good at cloaking and scrambling his conversations to the point where we need one of those Navajo code breakers to know anything about what's happening before he is good and ready to tell us. Being Dakota Sioux, I gather very little, so I concentrate on my driving.

And on how quickly things can change here.

We were so . . . big. I don't mean in the sense that we were sizable and powerful as a military force, though there was that. More than that, we were substantial, this thumping column of machinery splitting through the center of this whole new place. We were like a part of the landscape, like we belonged here, in lieu of any visual cues telling us that we didn't. There were none.

Until those evil little birds.

And that's just how they seemed at first. We were thunder, they were whine. We were solid, they were wispy. We were *right here*, they were horizon speckle.

Until they flew right up our noses, straight into our heads.

I catch Commander Cowens's engine hitting high revs, and I'm sensing that it is not a subordinate or even a peer he's getting feisty with when he snaps into the phone, "That is exactly what I have been telling you helmet-heads all along. That approach is no longer gonna work anywhere, especially not here. . . ."

The conversation stops itself just like that, before it can get really good.

Because the action in front of us beats them to it.

"Aw, for the love of Pete," Wyatt calls as he sees the same thing we all see.

Pacifico raises his volume like an air raid warden cranking a siren, and here we go again.

Same thing, same formation, same blood-boiling scream, could even be the same planes, most of them, as they scorch toward us from that very same direction.

One difference is the response. We start firing like crazy at the planes just as soon as we can get a bead on them. Nobody's even waited for orders before going into full battle mode, probably too early.

"Slow it down!" Cowens screams. "Don't waste everything on out-of-range panic. You're doing their jobs for them! We'll be out of ammo before they even get here, and I can tell you *that* won't be a pretty sight."

It is at that very second that I find myself thinking like a coordinator instead of just some guy with a very simple specific role to carry out.

Supply. Holy cow. We have been met only once so far by supply trucks bringing us fuel, ammo, food, and all the stuff that goes *into* an assault vehicle before you can get anything out of one. And I am suddenly aware that we are overdue for the next rendezvous.

"Pace yourselves!" I blurt out.

"I'll handle this if you don't mind, Commander Bucyk," says the actual commander.

"Sorry, sir."

They are right over us again. The insane screeching, from above, from within. The tin-can-of-rocks sensation jars the tank senseless, again.

I swear I see the pilot's face looking right into my eyes, followed by the most humiliating instant of my life.

I look away.

As quick as humanly possible, I whip my face back to the spot but of course it's too late. He's gone, and he's done it and I broke. Coward.

I am furious, can feel my face flush, and secretly beg for that plane, that one, that 109 fighter right there, to come back. You. *You*. It doesn't matter if we get him, if he shoots me dead in the eye, it doesn't matter. He has to come back and give me . . . come back so I can *take it back*. And hold him still so he can die there, in the dirt, in front of my tracks where he will be crushed.

"Come on, come on, come on!" Logan is howling like a lunatic as a pair of them, a Stuka and a fighter, come in together, closer and closer, weaving among bullet hails and poorly shot shells, and he holds his fire, holds it longer, holds it beyond even when Cowens orders him loud enough to pop the lid off his own hatch.

"I said, *fire*, Logan!"

He finally fires.

It is beyond spectacular. I don't ever expect to see a shot as perfect as the one right there, where the nose of one beautiful seventy-five millimeter shell connects perfectly with the nose of an ME-109 German Luftwaffe fighter plane and creates the fiery chaos of the ages, right above the column of tanks, raining fire and debris down on all of us, making clangs and dents and divots of joy all up and down the line.

The Stuka banks off through the smoke, back toward the north, with the bulk of his comrades. But not before two more, farther back in our line, have been brought down. And not before, up ahead and not three tanks back, our guys take substantial bomb hits to go with the machine-gun rounds that are pockmarking everything in sight.

Far up ahead there has been some command decision, as I see the light tanks accelerate and put distance between them and us, no longer hanging back for whatever it was we were hoping solidarity would achieve.

It appears we are seriously fighting the Germans now for possession of Western Tunisia.

We are taking casualties. They are taking casualties.

There is a Luftwaffe pilot who took something from me. And then took it to the grave.

The column has stopped. Cowens is involved in frantic radio talks. The other two guys up there are growling like bears while Pacifico sounds the siren.

I stare straight ahead and find myself worrying the scapular between my fingers and thumb.

We don't move.

It's decided we will sit right here in the middle of the desert, dig in, and wait.

Supplies are not far off, and right behind them are artillery units, with infantry to follow shortly.

"That is how it should be," Cowens says as we walk up and down the line, examining the damaged tanks just before night falls too dark to examine anything. "These units have to be blended. A bunch of tanks make a nice show of power, but they aren't nearly flexible enough to be carrying out major operations by themselves for long. Tanks shouldn't even be fighting tanks most of the time — we should be blowing up other stuff and supporting the foot soldiers. Finally we're breaking this parade up into smaller units, mixed units, spreading out, fighting smart."

"I wish you were in charge," Wyatt says to the commander.

The commander responds with something that becomes a sort of low-key motto for our crew.

"I wish General GSP was here."

That would be George S. Patton.

"Only two guys on our side who really know what tanks are all about, me and him," Cowens says as we finish our inspection and he does a crisp heel-turn to lead us back toward the evening's bunk-down. "And I have no interest in being the boss, so it's gotta be him."

It's fortunate for us that Commander Not-the-Boss is kind of engrossed in his philosophies at the moment, as his minions exchange glances and grins that he might not approve of if he should suddenly turn around.

I'm walking alongside Pacifico, just behind Logan and Wyatt. My assistant driver is still not quite with us, and I allow us to lag behind a little.

"Hey," I say low, just between us, "you all right?"

He keeps walking, looking straight ahead with his expression giving up nothing and his voice giving up less.

"Hey," I say again, elbowing him in the side for punctuation.

He turns to me quickly this time. "Hey," he says with at least a portion of his goofy smile.

We keep walking, but I know he's not quite correct, so I keep staring at him. He looks away.

I grab his right arm with my left hand, and he looks back, with sad worry.

"I'm not hearing stuff. Not too good," he whispers. I realize now, he's whispering louder than someone who can hear whispers.

"Aww," I say, squeezing his arm harder. "Kid. Kid, you have to —"

"No. Bucyk, no. I'll be fine. It's not completely . . . and it'll get better. The ear that I listen to you guys with is better, anyway, so —"

I can see now that he's even favoring one ear, tilting his head a bit to the right. I squeeze the daylights out of

that arm and there's more where that came from if necessary. "Go home, pal. You didn't want to be here,
anyway. You did your bit, and then some. Go home."

The other guys don't notice when we stop. Pacifico
yanks his arm away, plants himself in my face, and
squeezes my upper arms now. No contest, frankly,
as my pal may be stout of heart, but he's fairly limp
of limb.

"No, I didn't want to be here," he says. "But I don't
want to go home. I belong with you guys, and that's
where I want to be now. You say anything to mess that
up, I'll beat your brains in."

I can only hope he takes it in the nicest possible way
when I cover my mouth with my hand to shield his sensitive eyes from the laugh he can only half hear.

He gives me the full-watt, ear-to-dud-ear grin that
could sell me a lot of stupid ideas.

"Fine," he says, "but I would shoot you."

"Fair enough," I say. "But I'll be watching you. If
you can't cut it . . ."

He nods, and pulls me along to catch up with
our team.

His attitude being what it is right now, his whole
head would have to fall on the floor in front of me
before I'd want him off the crew.

"Everything good?" Cowens says as we find him waiting outside the Sherman.

"Good-good," I say.

"Good," Pacifico says.

They both start climbing up to hunker down for the night. I slip casually around to the other side first and get way up close to eyeball Pacifico's side of the tank in the low light.

There must be forty small dents, near-penetration pockmarks, in a semicircle beside where his head would be. Looks like the outline of a giant ear.

It's a funny notion, lying awake through the night when you're not even lying down to begin with. Tossing and turning? Hardly. I've lost the ability to identify exactly what sleep is now, anyway. I am never fully asleep, never fully awake during the nights when the five of us are propped up in our cramped steel dormitory. The difference between what you are dreaming and what you are thinking becomes blurred. If there is even a difference.

Tonight I'm pretty sure it's mostly awakeness and mostly thoughts. You learn early on in battlefield life that the Army itself never fully goes to sleep. There is a constant low hum of something going on, an engine, a clanking, murmurings and motion sounds that never let you feel alone no matter how much you might want to.

Not that I could feel that way, anyway. He's been with me tonight. My Luftwaffe pal. The pilot who stared me down. Broke me down. And has now decided to move in with us right here in my tank. My Sherman. Did he die back there? Didn't he? Does it matter, if he's gotten in here?

It's close to daybreak when I hear a sound that sounds a little different. It's a motor, but it's not a motor I recognize.

I quietly push the hatch open to go explore.

"Where's your sidearm, Bucyk? And your helmet?"

I am startled, and it serves me right for thinking that the commander would not be vigilant.

"Oh, sir, I'm just —"

"Not without your weapon, you're not. Never."

"Yes, sir," I say. I grab my helmet and strap on my pistol before exiting.

I knew it was a foreign sound, and foreign it is.

"Morning," I say as I approach the vehicle. I had only heard about these guys before now, never seen one. The Long Range Desert Group (LRDG) vehicle the Brits have been operating in Egypt since the early days of the war. It's a handsome little brute, the nose looking

like an old Chevy farm truck and the rest being all camouflage and heavy artillery. They operate like free
agents, advance scouts buzzing all over the desert finding out what everybody's doing, then disappearing
again to make use of the intelligence.

"G'day," says the guy who's in the navigator's seat.

"Morning," says the driver, nodding.

"What brings you guys to our neighborhood?" I ask.

"Just having a li'l looky-round," the navigator says,
"see what we can see, know what I mean?"

It is an accent I haven't heard a lot of. "Australian?"
I say.

"Get it right, mate, or could be trouble. Kiwi. New
Zealand."

"Right. Sorry."

"Yes, well, it's time," the driver says. Then he stares
silently, sort of right over my shoulder. That accent, I
recognize: British officer.

"Where you going?" I ask the navigator.

"Just beyond that bluff there. Gettin' a quick dig-
around among the wreckages you made. Never know
what useful stuff you might find."

"Oh," I say, sounding like an excited kid, knowing I
sound like an excited kid, not caring that I sound like
an excited kid. "Could I tag along?"

The New Zealander looks at the Englishman, who looks in the direction of the bluff. There must be some kind of communication between them that I can't read because the Kiwi comes back to me and says, "Where's your commander?"

"Ah," I say, gesturing indirectly toward the Sherman, "he's sleeping."

"Guess that means the answer's yes, then," the guy says cheerfully, and I jump into the back of the vehicle just as it's pulling away.

Sure enough, when we get to the other side of the bluff there are two downed German planes, a Stuka and an ME-109, both crumpled, singed, and embedded in the earth. We park the LRDG and approach the Stuka. We walk all around it, over the one intact wing, around to the cockpit. There is no sign of the pilot anywhere. Not inside, not in the area. He could have landed anywhere. Good.

I leave them there as they pick apart the cockpit, pulling the control panel to pieces, looking for whatever secrets the Desert Group looks for. I approach the 109. The pilot's cage has been torn right off. But as I climb up on the wing and look in, I see the deceased pilot himself has miraculously remained in there. He is in a very strange position, though, kind of reclined with a blanket under him, but with one arm up over his head as if in a half surrender. His face is bloody chopped tomato pulp, turned like he's looking toward his own shoulder. His teeth are all knocked out, which is easy to see because he appears to be frozen in mid scream. Good.

"Don't touch," the British officer snaps as the two of them march toward me.

Was I touching? I wasn't aware of touching. Maybe I was. I look at my hands.

They are up on the plane now with me, on the opposite wing. I feel like a consultant surgeon watching them work. They examine the pilot for a few seconds before the Brit decides it's okay to start on the instrument panel, and the Kiwi pulls the pilot up toward him.

In a snap, I see two guns. They flash, either side of the pilot, as a second pair of German arms sprout up from underneath the first pair. Both Desert Groupers duck the bullets just as the second pilot's face appears, gritting, snarling, all teeth and hate, and my pistol is already in my hand and I pump a bullet right into his temple and I see that face and I recognize that hateful face and I pump a second and a third shot into his head before he even can fall all the way back again and under the other man once more. Blood pumps out of the guy's head like it's going to make a bath right there in the cockpit.

There is a whole lot of silence in the desert now. I can smell the work of my gun.

I see the men of my crew going about their morning business as the LRDG vehicle pulls up to about fifty yards away. "This will be close enough," I say. The British officer doesn't need to hear it twice. He stops. I hop out and walk around to the navigator's side of the vehicle. From the driver's seat I get a silent salute, which I return. From the Kiwi I get a big grin and a pretty hard slap on my neck. He grabs my ear under the helmet and shakes my head all around.

"Now that was some killing, mate."

I don't say anything, but I do nod when he releases me to do so.

"Let us know when you want to join up with the Desert Group. Anytime."

I hear the Chevrolet engine growl as they motor away behind me and I head toward my own desert group.

I can't wait to get there. To get into my tank, where I belong. I fight for my country, and now I'm pretty sure

I could also fight for New Zealand, but I know my place, my war, is in that Sherman with my guys.

I watch Commander Cowens all the way as he watches me walk home.

"Did you find what you were looking for?" he says, fatherly, as I climb up the front of the tank to my hatch.

"I did, sir," I say. "Yes, I did."

CHAPTER EIGHT
Peaks and Passes

We are traveling now with three companies — about sixty tanks in all. We're supported by two artillery platoons, but as of yet no infantry.

It feels like lighter going, in terms of speed and flexibility, but to be honest it's still hard to get a read on what the big picture is. Everybody talks about reaching Tunis as the big prize. The British Eighth Army has been driving the German and Italian forces up from the south, and we are coming in from the west, with the idea that we are going to combine those pressures to shove the enemy up against the coast, into the sea, and off of Africa's back once and for all. When we have done that, then the whole Mediterranean is ours, with staging areas for operations from east to west and uninterrupted supply lines that will really turn things around in Europe.

That's the theory, anyway, and Tunis is the brass ring.

But from here? We're never sure what's around the next bend, over the next little hillock. And communication among units, battalions, divisions, armies, branches, allied *nations*, seem for all the world to be making our task more confused, rather than less. It's all certainly frustrating the person immediately above me in the vast, vast, vast chain of command.

"Look at that, now," Cowens says as we slog through a surprisingly horrible rain, over nearly impassable mud tracks. All our vehicles are sashaying their way along, trying desperately to hold a steady path toward wherever we are headed. I now see firsthand what parched, arid land looks like once it's pounded with bucketing rainfall, and it ain't fun. What we know for certain is that Tunis is on the other side of a seriously imposing backbone of mountain range that practically divides this country, Tunisia, in two, right down the middle. We also know that the far side of that range is mostly Axis-held. As for what befalls us between here and there, that is anyone's guess, but so far it has been a series of surprises, pleasant and otherwise.

We have had a number of skirmishes. Mostly held our own. A little more than held our own, in fact. All things considered, the kids have been doing all right.

"So, we're taking this hill blindly, I guess," says Cowens. He's having one of his surlier days.

"Unless you tell me otherwise, sir," I say. "The way I see it, my command structure extends as far as you. Say the word and I stop, back up, do a backflip, you name it."

"Thank you Bucyk. You're a good soldier. But good soldiers follow orders, as you know, and my orders are to follow this line and so those are your orders, too."

"Will do, commander."

I reach to my right, slap Pacifico on the leg, and steer to the top of the hill with the rest, and following their formation, I pull up and alongside the previous tank and survey the scene.

"Oh, my goodness, me," Logan says. "Is it my birthday? Wyatt, load, man, load."

"Sir?" Wyatt asks, appropriately.

"Hold on, hold on, wait for instructions," Cowens says, grabbing up the radio.

We can *try* to hold on.

There is a gentle slope before us, descending into a valley along a river. Just on the other side of that river is a small, secluded, packed German airfield. There are a few planes taking off and landing, but virtually no defensive presence that we can see beyond that.

Cowens, still on the phone, speaks in the kind of abnormal calm you use when you don't want to wake somebody or you're afraid of disturbing your own fantasy.

"The artillery is setting up right where we are," he says. "In a few seconds, when we get the word that they are set, the tanks roll and lay down a line of fire the whole way. Load up, gentlemen. . . ."

I see scores of Messerschmitts, and Stukas, and ME-109s, mostly just sitting there. They don't notice us at all yet, nested in with the trees here on the hill.

"Ready . . ."

The sound of the 81-mm mortar fire is like the starting gun on a race, and we are off, down the hill with a beautiful barrage arcing over from behind us and a glorious explosion of panicked terror before us.

I lean into the levers just as hard as I can to get us across the field and to the riverbank as fast as possible. All the while my boys are just pounding everything they've got into laying waste to anything that moves on the other side of that river, and anything that doesn't.

It's satisfying like nothing else. There has just been this percolating, burning hatred of these aircraft that's been growing by the hour, especially since we crossed over into Tunisia. They seem to always have the advantage, to always bring down fire and havoc and then almost every time get away before you can get your hands on them. German air superiority has just been so complete that is seems like the situation is entirely devoid of fairness, and that's how crazy it's gotten, that I am looking for fairness in battlefield situations.

Mortar shells are landing, one after another, blowing up aircraft where they sit. The thin line of troops they mobilize to defend are up and shot down as fast as they can get to the fence. Our shells are pounding the installation's buildings right back into the sand they came from.

The rain has stopped by the time we sit on the river's edge, but it's all still muck, and running water, and blood.

"Switch," I say to Pacifico's good-ish side.

I get nothing.

Check that. I get *furious*.

I grab sweet Pacifico with both of my hands and heave him, like a butcher with a dead carcass, out of his seat and over onto my side. I can feel him crash and crumple as I jam him into my seat and force him onto the controls. Right now I don't have the time or the humanity for niceties as I apply myself to the task of killing.

"Switch!" I roar, just to be sure he gets my point.

He doesn't need to hear it three times, fortunately. He stares straight ahead, holding the steering levers like they are his life. I am at the machine gun, sighting through my scope, locating the right plane and riddling it, murdering it beyond dead, then turning to the two valiant monsters who are right beside it, each down on one knee, taking aim at me that I can see so, so clearly in their eyes. I kill them, two of them, and I know it, and they know it, and when they fall I am looking into them just as they are looking into me and I keep on firing. *Take that with you*, I say, as they go all the way down and I shoot them even further, down into the next world. *Take that with you, if you don't mind.*

Pacifico pats my shoulder, just like I do when he's in this seat. I turn to him, and I mouth more than vocalize.

"That's *one*," I say, holding up an index finger between us. "I don't expect there to be a *two*."

He just shakes his head, no, no, no and sad, sad, sad, and right now he seems more scared of me than he does of the bad guys.

We're not Navy — thank goodness — but waters seem to dictate our movements. First it's coastline, now this river. We receive our orders to follow it, once we get across, follow it south, even though Tunis is not south, and the mountain range that must be crossed is not south. But there is something like a vision emerging, that we need to spread this line of ours a bit. And so we do, and we do so, if I may say so, fairly successfully.

We make fairly steady progress running parallel with the river, keeping the infamous mountain range to our left. Operating almost like an independent army, our three tank units and two artillery platoons are well matched for most configurations we run into. We have more firepower than the light tank and infantry units we come across. We have more versatility, options, and, frankly, speed than the heavily armored outfits. We have managed to avoid direct confrontations with any of the more legendary elements of the armored Afrika Korps, with their panzers and antitank high velocity 88-mm cannons.

Then, as we near Christmas, we get a present. Or possibly become one.

In a situation not unlike when we rolled right on top of the unguarded airfield, we reach another lightly wooded rise at just about the southernmost point of what is our established line of defense. The run south from here is going to be a long stretch of fairly unknown territory all the way down to Kasserine, about two hundred miles away.

With this already on everyone's minds, we are maybe a little bit distracted when we all but run into the flank of a showdown already in progress.

An American light tank company, frighteningly isolated somehow out here where they don't belong, have been confronted by a group of eight panzers, each fitted with a monster 88-mm cannon. Our Shermans carry only 75s, and our light tanks — like I drove in the Carolina Maneuvers — are equipped with only these stubby 37-mm pop guns, meaning this figures to get real ugly, real fast.

As the panzers approach across the field, I am aware once again that stealth and geography are the most potent weapons in the whole war business. We are shaded, on a low rise so that while unseen, we still have a good shot.

Commander Cowens gets the word in his ear and this time there is no setup.

"Fire!"

We unload, the tanks pounding down the 75s, the 81-mm mortars doing their bit, and the other artillery platoon unveiling their latest greatest, the British-made twenty-five-pound shells, which are every bit as bruising as they sound.

We surely catch the panzers by surprise, because the confusion is written all over their moves. Big turrets turn like petrified elephants with arthritis, and they can't seem to decide who's going to shoot up at us and who's going to clobber the little M-3s. Three of them, then four, apparently decide that we are the bigger problem, and then a fifth joins in as we continue to hit them with our best. We've scored a number of hits already, and the retaliation is coming. Because we are doing damage down there. One twenty-five-pounder has hammered right into the side of one panzer, just above the sprocket. It's penetrated, and there is fire. Fire in a tank of any size is lethal, and crew are bailing right out onto the field.

Puuuh-whooosh-ppooom!

Holy moly. One of those 88s sails no more than three feet over our heads, and blasts a tree behind us. The tree is gone. The air is gone; we could feel it leave before the thing even hit.

Those guns are as advertised.

But we have the leverage, and it's working. We're rocking them, holding and pressing and winning.

Puuuuwhoooom-boom.

It's a total crater that's created, in the earth on the downslope just ahead of my tank and we are now mud-sledding forward.

"Bucyk!" Cowens yells.

I'm already on it. I am pulling back hard, and the Sherman's engine is grinding it out with me. But the tracks are having no luck getting a purchase in the muddy earth as it floods away from us and we move forward, down into that valley of death. I hear the guys gasping, trying not to, yelling me encouragement, but the more I try to make the tank maneuver, the more it gets away, and we are going down.

The light tanks, which have been offering the panzers little more than annoyance and distraction, now move like a crack, coordinated veteran unit. They charge as one toward the big beasts, who catch on a tick too late and struggle to swing back their way.

I notice, now, the only negative I can see in these creatures. They have so much top-heavy power that rotating the turret is a ponderous machination. Their machine guns rattle the smaller tanks, but it's not enough. Half the light tanks hold back, while the other half make a bold run around the left flank, opposite us, pulling panzer fire along with them. The light tanks, crazy courageous as they are, have come dangerously close before running wide.

The panzers look like they are swinging bats, but the bats are telephone poles.

They are open now, vulnerable, caught between the medium tanks up high and the light tanks below. And to my thrilled amazement, I watch while we slide forward down that muddy slope, and all the inferior machines lay it all in there, throwing every ton of ordnance at them, relentless as a pack of hyenas and just as deadly.

We take down the great beasts, destroying two, and watch the rest retreat across the field into their safe territory, backing up all the way with their 88s in our faces but their tails between their legs.

We may just know what we're doing here.

My Dearest Dope,

Of course we can have them over to dinner. I'll start preparing for them right away. Should it be in the dining room, with the good china and crystal, or maybe something more informal on the patio? They sound more like a patio bunch, I think. That way, you can be out there barbecuing, with the dogs and Little

Roman scurrying about in the sunshine while you and your pals tell all your old war stories.

I'm playing with you, of course. I'm not sure how much time there is for playing over there but no matter how much time there is it's not enough. Your friends sound like a grand group of guys, and I have been picturing them in my head already. I think it might be fun if I sketch them for you before you come home, and then we can see how close I got when we can finally compare. My drawing is not very good, but we'll all get a great laugh out of it, I'm sure. I'm thinking Commander Cowens looks like Gary Cooper. Or maybe Alan Ladd. Am I in the ballpark? Gosh, I hope so. (Just kidding. Mostly.)

Speaking of Hollywood, I went out to the pictures twice last month, which I haven't done at all since you left. But since two of the big new features were called Road to Morocco and Casablanca, I thought I should have a look at what you've been up to. From here it appears that it's either very silly, or very romantic over there. Which certainly contradicted the newsreels that ran just before the films.

I have to apologize for the briefness of my last letter. I was a bit emotional. I meant what I said, though.

I hope the enclosed clipping makes up for it. I think it's wonderful that the Eastern Shore Sportswriters Association continues to hold their annual banquet, don't you? And that players the likes of Jimmie Foxx and Bill Nicholson make the time to appear at someplace as glamorous as the Easton Firehouse. But that's Maryland folk for you. (I underlined the part where they mentioned your name. Knowing your newfound modesty, I wasn't sure you would locate it on your own. I was shamelessly proud on your behalf, however.)

My experience with the WAAC has been about as thrilling and fulfilling as it could be, short of my actually being the pilot I wanted to be. Roman, I am an air traffic controller now, at the Newcastle, Delaware airfield. It is demanding and important work, and I am deeply involved in the WAFS program that I signed up for to begin with. Guiding those pilots safely in and out of this busy airstrip every day makes me feel a part of both teams (the Auxiliary Ferrying Squad as well as the Army Auxiliary Corps). I wish I had time to describe everybody here, but I'm sure you already get what I mean.

One's team. We appreciate true teamwork, you and I.

We are great team players, are we not?

We'll be a great team ourselves, when the dust finally settles on all this.

All my love,
Corporal Hannah

P.S. Don't worry about those stripes of mine. There is no rank between us.

My Dear Hannah,

Things are going very well here. Constant progress, and I am comforted by my scapular, and thoughts of who gave it to me, on a daily basis.

As you know, I cannot say too much about what we are up to right now. You know in general terms about where I am, but I can't be more specific than that right now. Let's just say that I can see the goals, and I can see our clear and steady progress toward them. I think if a soldier has those two things then he should be able to do his job effectively, and if he can't then it's his own fault.

My crew continues to be a top-notch bunch, dedicated to the right fight. We are all determined that we will see it through to the liberation of the world from the mess that it's in. Commander Cowens fought with the Abraham Lincoln Brigade on the Republican side of the Spanish Civil War. He says that whenever he catches a fascist he bites their head off like cats do with birds. I know it sounds unpleasant, but the rest of us have agreed that we are looking forward to seeing it. Once, anyway.

I will admit, though, that the road is long, and it will test a man. But as long as I know that you are at the end of that road (with a few significant stops along the way for me to see to some overdue business with a certain bunch of mugs who've had it coming to them), then I will step lightly along it.

I hope it is all right that I take this as my turn to be brief. Just think of all the stories I'm holding back right now, that I can thrill you with someday soon.

I had not heard about Bill Thomas, so I am glad you let me know. Bill was a good man, and a good hitter.

I'm extremely proud of you joining the WAACs. If there's one person who could win this thing from the Eastern Shore, it's you. WAAC 'em good for me, soldier.

Humbly yours (how'm I doin'?),

Roman

I would never lie to Hannah. Unless I felt it was for the best.

I didn't lie when I told her it was steady progress. It was, at the time.

But as of right now, it's more like the old joke: It's not a lie, it's just a truth that hasn't happened yet.

We have gotten bogged down. In the unreliable weather, and in the ever-shifting arrangements and alignments that seem to be standard operating procedure when it comes to multination warfare in the north of the African continent. If such a thing as standard operating procedure existed here, which it seems not to.

"This is how it's going to go on forever, if somebody doesn't take this thing by the reins," Commander Cowens howls as we hump along yet another uneven, crater-holed track, on the way to another Tunisian outpost that's supposed to be important but turns out to be just as indifferent to us and the global situation as the last one. My driving skills are getting sharper all the time, but I'm not sure anything else about the team is at the moment. There is a frustrating, repetitive futility to the days now, which are stretching way beyond what we expected the Tunisian campaign to entail. Stuff that we had gotten used to being accomplished within days is now taking us months.

Months.

Geographically, we've moved a lot since we crossed into the country in November. We are well onto the eastern side of the Atlas Mountains, which was one of our primary objectives. But it seems the farther we get, the more II Corps gets watered down by higher command trying to cover and hold more and more positions with the same numbers of troops, artillery, and armor.

"Leave it to Lloyd," Logan chirps, launching one of our new and dangerous games for killing time — provoking Cowens.

"Oh, General Ward, too," Cowens says. "Don't forget Ward. He's in charge of the division, remember. And the only thing worse than being a know-nothing numbskull like Fredendall, is being the guy who stands there nodding at everything he's told to do by a know-nothing numbskull like Fredendall. Those guys won't be satisfied until every little peak and outcropping in this whole region is occupied by one infantryman, one vehicle, and a cat."

The crew roars. We do love Cowens's increasingly frequent fireworks displays. And they do pass the time.

"Maybe we should send Lloyd a postcard," Pacifico pipes up, leaning his good ear hard into the action. "Tell him what a fascinating country this is, and invite him to visit sometime."

I lean over and punch his shoulder. Give him the approval nod. We're very into visual communications down here on the lower level these days. I point at my eyes, then his, then mine again. *I'm watching you*, is one of the intended messages. The other is, *use your eyes for ears if need be.* He smiles goofy and repeats my eyes-eyes-eyes maneuver.

"Great idea," Wyatt says.

"Nah," I say. "The postage would be astronomical."

"I wish General GSP was here!" bellows Logan.

"GSP!" we chant. "G! S! P! . . ."

But in the middle of a freezing February night, we get an order that sounds right away like it means something. We are to haul it to a place called Djebel Hamra, which doesn't mean much to anybody, but is about fifteen miles to the west of a town called Sidi Bouzid.

There seems to have been a big problem in Sidi Bouzid.

Two whole panzer divisions with about 140 tanks have basically spent the day slapping the daylights out of big sections of II Corps. The result at the end of the day was a retreat — I have trouble even getting that word out — of our guys to Djebel Hamra. But not before suffering whopping losses of men and artillery. And more than forty tanks.

And they left behind several companies of infantry, stranded on high ground scattered at spots around the town. Stranded without armor.

"Well," Commander Cowens says with grim and humorless purpose, "I don't suppose we're ever going to feel more needed than we feel right now, huh, fellas?"

"Hold on, troops, we're coming!" Logan shouts. "Guns a blazin'!"

"Guns a blazin'!" we echo one at a time, each guy a little louder than the one before. A mighty column of words.

When we reach Djebel Hamra, handsome little plateau that it is, it seems clear that nature built it mostly as a viewing station for the serious action of Sidi Bouzid.

Turns out it is a long, flat fifteen miles between the two towns.

It's probably good that we barely have time to think about it before the combined mechanized forces are sent into the counterattack.

It begins almost instantly.

The air is filled with fighters and bombers flaunting the German control of these skies. We are mercilessly strafed and dive-bombed as we hurtle across the field toward Sidi Bouzid. We defend ourselves as much as we can, as much as we can get away with, really, but we know as well as they do that this is just to slow us down from getting to the real punch-up.

Still, it is hauntingly similar to all the lethal harassment we have endured along the road to getting this far. Logan is screaming murder in every direction, firing rounds just to keep them honest while saving his shells for the big game. Pacifico has gone back to his scary singing, but if that's helping him then I have nothing to say about it. The noise everywhere is, again, a battle all its own, and I am aware how much I have come to despise the part of warfare that rains from the sky.

"Is this it, commander?" Wyatt calls out, sounding like a scared-of-the-dark kid asking his dad to make everything right.

"This is it, kid. You good?"

Pause. Even with all the insanity of sound, we can hear him take his deep, brave breath.

"I'm good, sir."

"Good! Here we go!"

We *go* before we even know it.

While we are bearing straight ahead, looking straight

ahead, boring into the heart of Sidi Bouzid and the first tanks there we can see straight ahead, all the thunder in the universe suddenly cracks open on either side of us.

It looks like the entire bulk of a whole panzer division has materialized on each flank, and opened up on us with those monstrous 88-mm cannons. We were expecting to overcome their bigger, higher-powered machines with our numbers, but we look to be wrong on that score. We are coming with around a hundred light and medium tanks total, but the Germans have brought at least fifty percent more, and bigger, and there is a belly-of-the-beast feeling to this already that will make a man either sick to death or make him more man than he ever thought he could be. Like a sweaty giant cooling himself on both cheeks, they have circled around and fanned out so breezily that we are almost surrounded before we start. We penetrated deep before they even began to fire, and that mainly served to cut us off from much of the force almost instantly. We did just what they wanted us to, and they were probably waving at us as we sailed past.

Our tanks are blowing up already. There is chaos. The air attacks are just as serious as any of the isolated attacks we've endured over the months, but in the face of this onslaught they hardly seem to amount to anything worth our time.

But everything here is worth our time, if we only had the time, and the firepower, to deal with it.

"Where am I shooting?" Pacifico screams, frozen.

"Straight ahead, just like I told you way back."

He remains frozen. "Where am I shooting?" he screams again.

I lean over and slap him crisply with the back of my hand. He looks at me, shocked.

I point where I'm driving, though I don't know where I'm driving. "Like I told you. I'll aim the tank and you shoot straight ahead."

He starts peppering away at whatever it is I'm driving us into.

"We're going right flank, Bucyk, *hard*," Cowens calls. "Stay in formation with our group, right on the shoulder of number one there. Good. There you go. Here we go. We can do this, boys. We fight smart, we fight right, we win."

"Yes, sir!"

That may have been me shouting that but I honestly don't know.

This is already the sum of all the fights we have fought so far. The panzers and Tigers I see, up close now, are brutes. We are dwarfed, in armor and fire-power, as I pull up hard on the levers and we stand to fight.

"Yeeeahhhh!" Logan is screaming, with some kind of rhythm, as Wyatt feeds and he fires. He's keeping us confident, and keeping Wyatt in sync by doing it, but it's already failing.

There is carnage on this field. We are overmatched. The only thing keeping this contest a contest is the maneuverability of the Sherman. It's pretty fleet for thirty-eight tons, but they have the size and the numbers and the position. So we dodge, and we fire, and we dodge, and we fire. We draw fire, make them miss, make them waste, and as of now that feels like we're doing something.

We all cheer when Logan scores a direct hit that seems to at least have stunned one Tiger into a silence that I hope is permanent.

My hope is dashed as that Tiger singles us out and I sense it just before he unloads, *bu-hoom*, and I am already reversing before he can change his sight. The shell misses us but scores, brutally, deafeningly, on one of our guys that was already put out of its misery earlier.

Eventually it is only the size of the force we have sent that gives the impression of an ongoing, viable fight. I've seen vehicles and mobile artillery of all description rolling in to support us as the battle has ground on, and most of them are now just so much more meat for the German grinder.

We are still slugging, firing everything we've got as fast as we can. We're absorbing more small arms hits, avoiding the larger ones by smaller and smaller margins, when the referee finally calls it.

"Pulling out!" Cowens hollers while still on the phone. "I said we're retreating, Bucyk. Move this machine, now, back toward Djebel Hamra. We're regrouping. Stay in formation with our group."

Regrouping.

I swing behind Number One tank. Number Five pulls behind me. That's our group now.

There is silence inside the Sherman as we flee, at maximum speed, leaving defeat and a whole lot of United States Army on the field behind us.

There have been retreats before. But now it's us.

And that was just the beginning of running the wrong way for us.

Having lost another forty-six tanks that day on top of the previous losses, we are definitely licking our wounds when we are ordered to withdraw all the way back to Kasserine Pass. This represents about two months' worth of backtracking over a matter of days. The First Armored Division is today ninety-eight tanks, fifty-seven half-track armored vehicles, twenty-nine artillery pieces, and five hundred fine fighting men poorer than it was at the beginning of yesterday.

Good thing there are no yesterdays in this game.

The pass is a major strategic location, a two-mile-wide cut in the Atlases that represents one of the primary throughways between the major contested sectors of the Tunisia campaign. It feels like an important assignment. And for once they appear willing to pull a lot of forces together for a single goal.

It looks something like a dry-gulch Old West frontier town as we roll through the dusty core of the pass. British and American infantry, artillery, and mechanized units are all set up in every conceivable spot, from the flats to the ridge tops, to little bluffs of rock jutting out halfway between the two. This landscape is harsh, stark, wicked. It looks less like any natural piece of planet Earth I ever imagined, and more like a place that has been pulverized, smashed, and crushed over and over and then the rubble pushed around into mounds and gullies with giant bulldozers for some big toddler god's amusement. It looks like silence to me, this terrain.

It's been a very quiet trip this time. Quietest extended stretch since we all met, I'd say.

"This appears promising," I say, regarding the variety of company we are now keeping.

"Hnnn," Cowens grunts.

"You disagree, I take it?"

"Look at them," he says. "Really look at them. Their faces, their movements."

I am driving standing up. I have my head popped out of the hole, as do Cowens and Pacifico. We must look like a traveling prairie-dog hutch.

"You can smell it. This is still a hundred little armies, rather than one big one. The only difference here is that we're placed a little closer together."

I couldn't see all that, really, much less smell it. Until Commander Cowens pointed it out.

This would probably be a good time to be able to doubt his senses, but I still haven't developed that skill. And if we are being honest, we'd consider ourselves partly responsible. As we have moved, through our training, our sailing, our deployments, and battles, we have become a little army ourselves, the five of us. Our tank, our world.

I just figured that was a good thing, and the way it was supposed to go. It sure has made our crew a'fighting unit in the best sense.

"Sometimes you can be awfully negative, commander," Pacifico says, pointing his hearing ear menacingly at the boss.

Cowens manages a bit of a chuckle.

"You might be right, kid. I'll have to keep an eye on that."

It's cold and windy up here in Kasserine country at night. It is black, as we sleep in the tank. We've seen tent camps set up all over the area, but we don't bother with that. This is what we do, our crew. I don't even know if I'll be able to sleep lying down when I get out of tank service.

"How come we don't get nicknames?" comes Logan's voice out of deep, deep left field, on the warning track.

"Which one of you nuts said that?" the boss groans.

"Me, sir, Logan."

"Fine. Your nickname is Nuts. Now, go to sleep."

"Okay, but doesn't everybody in the whole armed forces get a nickname at some point? Part of the experience, isn't it?"

Cowens sighs. "I thought Wyatt was in charge of nicknames."

Go on, kid, bite.

"Why's that, captain?"

The laughter is instant and spontaneously perfect, like a mean choir.

"Why's Dat?" Pacifico calls out, speaking for everybody.

"Very funny, *Nonna*," Wyatt calls back.

"Hey!" Pacifico says. "But, my *nonna* —"

"That leaves you, Bucyk," Cowens says, getting very much into the swing of it. "Since you all may very well have nicknames for me, but I very well better not hear them. You're up."

I almost forgot myself. I feel my smile unfurl.

"I already have a nickname, captain."

"Do share."

"The Captain. Since I was a kid. I've always been known as The Captain."

"Allll right," Logan says, clapping his hands and rubbing them together.

The other captain waits for the fuss to die down.

"Um, no," he says, mysteriously without explanation.

"He was a pro ballplayer," Pacifico says. "In the Red Sox system. Let's call him Teddy Ballgame."

There is another pause.

"Bucyk, are you telling us you were in pro ball?"

"I wasn't telling you that, but I guess I am now. Yeah, I was in the Red Sox system."

There is another pause. Cowens is a very skilled pauseman.

"It's settled, then. Bucyk's nickname will be *Liar.* Unless you prefer Pinocchio, because we're pretty flexible."

There is a lot of low-level, high-satisfaction laughter before it settles.

"Can I sleep on that, sir, and let you know my decision in the morning?"

"Sounds reasonable. Unless you wake up in the morning and tell us you're Franklin Delano Roosevelt."

"I'll try not to, sir."

"Good night, men," Cowens says, pulling the curtain down on our little show.

I am certain it is the first time he has called us that.

"Chief." Cowens's voice comes low from the silent night later.

"What's that?"

"Chief. I'd say that's the Sioux Indian version of Captain. I can't live with another Captain in the tank. But I can live with a Chief, I think."

It feels like getting DiMaggio's autograph. And his bat.

"Saves me a decision in the morning," I say. "Thanks. Good night, captain."

"Good night, Chief."

If I get no closer than this to the Medal of Honor, I'll have no complaints.

It feels almost familiar, the way the next week goes. Familiar because it's a lot like how Oran was, toward the latter part, when there was clearly some fierce fighting going on right around the corner, but it remained there, somebody else's business. We just figured all along everything would work out correctly for our side.

I still believe that.

But after a week the morning breaks, as it seems mornings tend to break in war, with an urgent call to get to a position about a mile from where we are, because Rommel's tanks are in our yard.

Like the vicious guard dogs we are, the bulk of the tank command flies in that direction. We have no idea what else is being sent in terms of manpower and machine-power, but there is enough of it around that we can be confident it will show, if it's not already there.

The old howl and snarl is back in the team as we race out to defend what we have, incredibly and in short order, come to feel is *our* place, our pass, our country, even.

This is right. This one feels right.

We are storming into the depths of the ravine, rounding the small foothill that was our cover, rushing to help out at the critical east entrance to the pass.

We come close to colliding with a company of light M-3 tanks from the battalion sent ahead of us, who are in full flight from a company of German Tigers.

As the M-3s rush past us, we open fire on their pursuers.

"How did they get here?" Cowens screams. "How did we not know?"

We cause the Tigers very little trouble as they are at high speed already, and before we know it we are running west instead of east, chasing the German tanks back into what we thought of as our base. It's occurring to me much too late that we are passing by machinery and bodies, freshly dead and dropped right here in our stronghold.

We are gaining ground on the Germans, feeling good about our chances as we pound rounds and shells into the tails of the running Tigers for a change.

"*This* is more like it, men!" calls the commander, reborn. "Run them down, Chief. Blow them into oblivion, Nuts!"

"Yes, sir! Yes, sir!"

It is our finest moment. We are fighting against the best now, and we are winning.

Bu-hoom bu-hoom bu-hoom bu-hoom.

Suddenly the all-too-familiar sound and feel of the 88-mm cannon is all over us, all around, and *coming* from all around.

"Holy . . . holy . . ." is the sum of the commands we get now from the commander.

"They're up top!" Logan howls as he swings his 75-mm gun up as straight as if he were going into anti-aircraft mode.

There is panic now in our tank.

"Wyatt, for cryin' out loud, load!" Logan screams. Then I hear thrashing around and finally Logan loads his own gun.

We have stopped short, to assess, and to dig in against . . .

"They've taken it," Cowens says evenly, surveying all sides through his scope. "They've done it. Look. During the night, they came in, and took the heights right away from us, both sides of the pass."

I use my own scope to check it, desperate to find him wrong for once. Just this once, please.

"It was a trap," Commander Cowens says. "A wonderful, brilliant, rotten trap."

"And here we are," I say, still looking past all the mounting, mounted evidence for a better outcome.

If it's up to Nuts Logan, anyway, we have nothing to worry about. He's loading and firing and loading and bellowing like there's no tomorrow.

"Bucyk," Pacifico says. "Bucyk," he says again, tugging on my arm when I fail to look down from looking up. The world is walls of deafening explosion, sound and shake, and it doesn't even matter anymore what direction it's coming from.

"What?" I say, like my pal is a nuisance keeping me from my stargazing.

He points straight ahead.

One solitary Tiger, all fifty-seven tons of tank, one of the beasts we were chasing and tail-whipping, has turned.

It is slowly — much more slowly than necessary — advancing on us, daring us, mousing us as it comes. When we were chasing the Tiger we were exploiting its only real flaw, a lack of straight-ahead speed. It's laughing now as it comes, showing us its 88-mm cannon looking as long as a football field, its front armor that is four inches thick.

I learned every detail from the great Tankist himself.

"Logan," Cowens says as coolly as any natural-born commander who ever lived. "You might want to forget about the hills, and fire on this guy." He points.

Logan swings down, he pounds a shell straight into the Tiger's face.

Wyatt jumps in, jams in the next round, and we fire.

So do they.

Pu-hoooom! Puuuu-hooooom!

My eyes are smoke and fire. My head is howling, crackling, the bone a thousand small fissures like a fat green log just when the ax splits it.

Their shell tears the entire turret right off of our tank. Sends it to the four corners, sends it up and down and nowhere. And I am lucky enough — just so, so lucky enough — to have the fraction of a fraction of a fraction of a second when I involuntarily whip my face away from the flash of the oncoming 88-mm shell. As a guy does in the face of an oncoming 88-mm shell, even if he is not a coward. And in doing this I am lucky enough to see the shell atomize the finest, truest, and rightest man I have ever met.

While he looks right at me.

CHAPTER NINE

Europe by the Toe

Pacifico and I looked up to the sky that day, like we were just two stupid rabbits coming up out of a hole. We just stared straight up into the sky from our turretless tank, our leaderless tank, our Loganless, Wyattless husk of a machine, and Pacifico would have gone right on staring if I hadn't grabbed him pretty much in a headlock and wrestled him up and out of there. We scrambled across the ground, on our bellies like they taught us in basic, and found ourselves a gigantic delicious boulder that was probably wedged against that Kasserine wall twenty-five wars ago.

We survived.

There was nothing wrong with either of us, by the standards of Army life in wartime, anyway. Certainly by the standards of that crew of five, in that tank on that day, we were shiny, new, fine.

Still, they thought it a good idea to get us out of harm's way for a little while, to get our gears some oil and reload for the fights to come.

They sent us on a holiday for three weeks while the fighting continued in Tunisia.

Our vacation destination was dear old home-sweet-Oran, Algeria.

My DEAR CORPORAL,

You should SEE ME NOW. I'm quite A goldbrick, lying ARouNd doing Not much of ANything on the PEACEful COAST of AlgeriA.

Then AgAiN, I'm the guy who MAdE it PEACEful, so I should be Able to ENjoy it SOME.

That wAS A joke, rather thAN A brAg. I will NEVER be boAStful ANd overconfident AgAiN. NEVER, EVER.

I'm here with my crew, on A mANdAtEd R+R, ANd R (that's rest, rehAbilitAtion, ANd, iN our CASE, SOME retrAiNiNg) before redeployment. PACifico, that's my crew.

The other guys won't be making it to diNNer, I'm AfrAid. PLEASE don't worry About me. Not A scrAtch, AS the SAying goes. AS it will AlwAys go for me. I'm very careful now, you know, family man and all.

Part of my ever-expanding education here has included a real understanding of irony (for the first time, I should confess). Commander Cowens always longed to serve under General Patton. Now, because of certain command failures that contributed to Commander Cowens now serving under Saint Peter, our corps has been put under the command of General George S. Patton. That is irony, yes? Have I got that correct?

Oh, forgot to mention, what's left of my crew is deaf. Or, extremely hard of hearing with a little more of it ebbing every day. He'll be good as long as we're together, but the feasibility of that may be slipping away. He's very concerned about the fate of Italy, so maybe if he gets in position to personally wrestle Mussolini to the ground sometime soon, he'll be able to retire with honor himself.

You are an air traffic controller now (I won't mention the stripes). Oh, how much we could use you here, because these skies are completely out of control.

I will write again soon, teammate. Or, with a little luck, we'll wrap this up and I'll see you even sooner.

                                                    Love,
                                                    Roman

    P.S. It's much more like <u>CASABLANCA</u> than <u>Road to Morocco</u> — they were kind enough to screen both for us since I've been back in Oran.
    And, you were right on the money about Commander Cowens and Gary Cooper.

Dear Roman,

    The more I hear, the more certain I am that you and your crew can topple tyrants wherever they show their rotten faces. I am believing in your Commander Cowens as much as you are, more and more all the time. His service in the Abraham Lincoln Brigade only confirms that you are lucky enough to be working with a true hero, of the country and of the world. And you can tell him I said so, even if it turns out he only looks like Mickey Rooney.

    Right behind the thought of seeing you again is meeting these great pals of yours. The country owes them much, but I owe them more.

    I know I should be writing more, but darling it just keeps

getting harder. I hope you understand, and know that I just want
to see you for real.

Love, and prayers,

and love,

Hannah

Boy, do I understand. Boy, oh boy, do I understand.

One surprise treat we get out of all this is that we are
retrained and reassigned to an M-3 Half-track Armored
Personnel Carrier. It's a beautiful atrocity of a thing. It
has the front end of a truck, with two wheels, and the
back end of an open-top tank, with tracks. Mounted on
top between the two is a big ol' .50-caliber machine
gun. The crew is only three — driver, gunner, and a
third man who rotates between both jobs as needed.
The half-tracks carry a load of ten troops, who get
delivered wherever the hot action and General George S.
Patton demands them.

When we return to Tunisia, I am driving that mag-
nificent creature, and Pacifico is my gunman. Our third
wheel is a guy named Martin, who happens to be a kind
of mutation between Logan and Wyatt. He sits quietly
with his hands in his lap in the assistant driver seat until
it's his turn on the firearms, at which point he turns

into Patton with a little more courage and a lot more volume.

The Sherman was an imperfect machine. That is probably as it should be, as a war should be fought by soldiers, with weapons in service to them, not *in place* of them.

I will love my M-4 for the rest of my life.

But this is where we belong now.

And the machine-gun perch on top of the M-3 half-track personnel carrier suits Pacifico much better.

Pacifico and I came back to a Tunisian campaign that seemed to have done all right in our absence. We left the field in February, returned in mid March, then delivered the right fighters to the right fights ten at a time until May 13, when all of North Africa, including 275,000 German and Italian prisoners of war, came into Allied hands.

By July, General Omar Bradley, who is also not bad, is leading II Corps, but General Patton is in charge of the entire Seventh Army, including two guys named Bucyk and Pacifico, as it invades Sicily.

We face an insanity of windy Mediterranean weather known as a *mistral*, causing a chaotic landing, followed by fierce fightback from the Italian forces, but we land

160,000 troops on the small island and no matter the blood and loss here, we feel it going our way, going north. ·

General Montgomery's British Eighth Army heads up the eastern flank of the island toward the ultimate destination of the port of Messina, which will once and for all secure all Mediterranean traffic for the Allies.

We head northwest toward the Sicilian capital, Palermo. It is brutal fighting we encounter, the kind only a desperate force wants to wage. For the first time, we have more of our planes buzzing overhead than theirs.

But there is no debate. This chapter of the war is closing, in our favor.

It takes a grueling two weeks before we do it, but we finally roll into Palermo victorious. We pause, drive slowly through the city, and find that, whatever Italian political sympathies were all along, in Palermo, on the streets, we are absolute heroes.

Martin is up top on the gun. He is pounding the roof as the troops we carry hoot like monkeys and shake hands with every last Sicilian they can reach.

It is euphoria.

I am giddy as I reach over to my copilot, and I slap his leg hard and several times.

Then I look up, at his face glistening, his chin and neck laminated with tears. I follow his gaze, out to the complete rubble of the city around these joyous people, the utter devastation. The punched-out windows in the grand hotels and churches. The crumblings of carved stone from buildings hundreds of years old lying like bread crumbs over the pavement everywhere you could see.

"*Nonna*," he says, wiping furiously at both eyes with the heels of both thumbs to make it stop. Like he has anything to be ashamed of.

I seize the hand closest to me, and won't let it go. And he cannot stop the crying.

As he should not.

The Allies are in their third day of bombing Rome. Rome, I have seen, in pictures. If Algeria and Sicily took my breath away, what will Rome do?

One day later, as we walk among the ruins and joy of Palermo, we get the news.

The Fascist government in Rome has fallen, and Mussolini has been arrested.

My best, and deafest, pal has not stopped weeping for twenty-four hours. I shout him the good news, which doesn't exactly help the sobbing situation.

"What now?" he shouts back, blubbering.

"Now?" I say. "Now, I drive you to the field hospital and turn you in. Your mission is accomplished, and you are going home, my friend."

He shakes his head vigorously until I seize it in both my hands.

"I say yes," I say. "And *Nonna* says yes."

Oh, jeez, now I've done it.

I lead the heaving mass of weep and honor and loyalty back to the half-track, I stuff him in, and I drive.

"What about you?" he asks, as I lead his deafness into the field hospital to rat him out.

"Me? I'm going to Berlin. I paid my ticket, and I'm not getting off 'til the ride's over. Can't let the general wipe out the Fascists all by himself, can I?"

"GSP!" he bellows, throwing himself at me in an unprecedented, not unwelcome, hug.

"GSP," I say into his not-so-good good ear. "And for us. I'll do it for all of us."

We hug, we nod, we don't look at each other, we hug a little longer, and together we make that infernal evil Stuka bomber noise until we can't take it anymore.

About the Author

Chris Lynch is the author of numerous acclaimed books for middle-grade and teen readers, including the Vietnam series and the National Book Award finalist *Inexcusable*. He teaches in the Lesley University creative writing MFA program and divides his time between Massachusetts and Scotland.